Tough Love

Heroes are People Too - Book 2

Cindi Annette

Strawberry Finch Ink Publishing

Cindi Annette

Copyright © 2020 by Cindi Annette
Digital ISBN: 978-1-7340419-2-7
Print ISBN: 978-1-7340419-1-0
Editing by: Danielle Chaloupka
Cover by: eBook Prep
Cover design by: Rennee Angeli Dasco
Published by: Strawberry Finch Ink Publishing

First Edition: March 2020

Contents

Cindi Annette

Dedication

To my husband John, who's been
the real hero for me over 47 years already.

Cindi Annette

Chapter 1

Tanner and Rachel had just arrived at the winery where Tanner grew up. Rachel was in awe. As she suspected, the place was huge in size and gorgeous in every way.

They had spent two glorious weeks in Kauai on their honeymoon. Now they were temporarily staying at the winery to help Tanner's parents prepare for the upcoming harvest. This would also give them time to look for their own house while staying under comfortable conditions.

"This place is beautiful," Rachel said, after getting out of the rental car and walking up the front steps. Not just any steps. They were made of layered red bricks that wrapped around the whole front entrance along with two large stone pillars. The effect reminded Rachel of the movie *Gone with the Wind*. The building had to be quite old but had been maintained beautifully. There wasn't a cracked brick in sight.

When she reached the top of the steps she stopped and turned around, taking in the view of the winery property. It was incredible. Green vines covered every field as far as her eyes could see. In each field, the grapes appeared to be different in color. She couldn't wait to find out why. She was sure it all meant something different as far as wine making was concerned but she didn't know what.

She noticed colorful flower gardens and fancy statues artfully scattered around the winery, making the place even more appealing. Just a short walk from the house there were convenient benches next to little gardens at various locations where the guests were sitting and enjoying their wine and snacks. It gave her an instant plan for the future, to bring her morning coffee and a book and to just sit, read and relax. The place was so charming that relaxing would come with ease.

The main visitor center looked very inviting. It had a sign that included its gift shop, wine tasting and wine sales. There was a full restaurant right next to it that had a sign mentioning live music and dancing. Rachel was excited to check that out as well.

She realized Tanner was right when he invited Ron to join them there. The winery had plenty of living quarters. She could see cabins dotting the back of the property, not to mention the huge main house which she was about to enter.

There were larger buildings she recognized from Tanner's description that must store the harvesting tractors, equipment, and the biggest building, she figured, would be where they made and stored the wine. All of these were set back from the main visitor center and restaurant yet close enough to see all the families enjoying themselves.

The place clearly had been there for many generations to be so large and elaborate. Workers were moving at a fast pace in every direction. Some were working in the vines, some driving tractors, while others were going in and out of buildings carrying supplies. All of the visitors seemed to be collected around the main building and restaurant.

This is no small winery. Rachel was impressed. She was even more impressed with Tanner after seeing the place. For his family to own a huge, successful business like this and for him to be such a humble man just enforced once more to her that she married the right man. She knew money could make a person hard sometimes, even if they don't try to be. But that wasn't Tanner.

"Yes, it's beautiful. Especially this time of year," Tanner agreed, lifting their heavy suitcases up the steps. "These seem a little heavier than usual," he said to Rachel with a wink. She grinned and replied, "Must be all of the souvenirs. You know I'm a light packer."

In all the splendor Rachel felt around her there was also a slight uneasiness. She sensed someone was watching them, but she saw no one. Then out the corner of her eye she saw movement in an upper bedroom window. A curtain had swayed. Someone had been watching but clearly didn't want to be seen.

Tanner opened the door and let out with a loud call, "Anyone home?"

"Tanner! Welcome home," Victoria called out. Tanner's mother came rushing through the swinging double doors from the kitchen. Her arms were open, ready to give Tanner and Rachel big hugs. She was thrilled for both of them to have finally arrived.

"I was just whipping up some lunch for everyone," she informed them.

"You should have let us pick you up at the airport, son, then you wouldn't have had to rent a car," Neil said, following Victoria out of the kitchen. He was anxious to see his son and new daughter-in-law again. They had loved Rachel the minute they met her at the wedding in Florida.

Anyone that made their son all smiles the way she did was good in their eyes. She had seemed sweet and bright from the moment they talked with her at the reception. However, they had to take a plane back to California the next morning and weren't able to get to know her very well. Big plans were being made for catching up on lost time now that Tanner and Rachel would be staying in their home for a while.

"No need Dad, I'm used to grabbing a rental car, it's easy. I've been doing it for years with my job, it's merely a routine," Tanner explained. He shook his father's hand and gave him a strong hug.

Tanner had been a very successful architect for office buildings and traveled the county for many years until marrying Rachel. Now he wanted to be a family man and restrict his work to designing in California only and the rest of his time working at the winery again.

"I can't wait to hear about your honeymoon in Kauai. Maybe you can tell us about it over lunch," Victoria suggested. She looked beautiful with her long, wavy, brunette hair. She had it all pulled up on the one side again, just like she wore it at their wedding. It was another thing that reminded Rachel of the movie *Gone with the Wind*. People wore their hair just like that in the movie. Rachel loved that look. She knew she was going to love it here, who wouldn't?

"The trip was great. We'd love to tell you all about it at lunch," Rachel replied, glancing Tanner's way and hoping he'd help with the stories. She turned her attention back to Victoria. "And thank you for letting us stay with you here."

"This is your home now. Tanner grew up here. You both will always be welcome here anytime you need a place to stay or just want to come visit, which I hope you'll do often," Victoria assured her with a welcoming smile.

Rachel's eyes casually roamed the interior of the house. It was a huge log home with a glowing wood interior. It had a vaulted ceiling and a rock fireplace big enough to cook an entire pig. The front room had two couches along with four very comfortable-looking recliners. The place was set up for lots of guests. Rachel figured Tanner must have grown up having lots of visitors in their home. No wonder he was so good with crowds.

"You could have used your old car to get around in instead of the rental," Neil mentioned to Tanner. "We still have it." It was Tanner's first car. It may have been old but it was still a sporty, dark green, reconditioned, sharp-looking Mustang.

"I thought Shawn would be driving it by now," Tanner replied, excited that his brother was at the driving age.

"I can't drive," a stern monotone voice came down from the top of the stairs, bringing silence to the room.

"Shawn!" Tanner called out, looking up the stairs. "Come on down here buddy. I want you to meet my wife," he said proudly as he waved his hand, gesturing for Shawn to come down the stairs. Tanner then reached out, pulling Rachel close to him, preparing for the grand introduction.

Shawn was a young man of seventeen and Tanner's only sibling. Tanner had told Rachel at their wedding reception that Shawn had serious phobias. He explained how his phobias had progressed to the degree that Shawn would not leave the house and now rarely left his room. Rachel could relate to phobias; she has some of her own. Tanner had witnessed her extreme fear of flying and other phobias since they met. None compared to Shawn's.

Tanner felt she might be able to relate with Shawn in a way that no one else could. Shawn was the other reason Tanner and Rachel had decided to move back to the winery. They had hopes of helping him with his phobias in some way, if they could. He had been this way for nearly a year now and they weren't sure if it was too late.

Shawn stood at the top of the stairs looking down at everyone. He was dressed in dark pants and a dark t-shirt. His hair wasn't long but looked unevenly cut as if Shawn had cut it himself and the rough on his face showed he could use a shave.

So that's who was looking out the window! Of course, Rachel realized. From what she heard, he lived in that room most of the time. *That window had to be his only connection to the world outside.* She glanced at Tanner's parents, wondering what their response would be to his attitude and appearance. Victoria looked anxious, as if praying Shawn would behave normally now that Tanner was back. Her face went glum when she saw that he still had on his dark clothes and depressed tone. He had ignored her request to clean himself up for the occasion. Neil looked at Shawn then down at the ground, crushed momentarily, as if exhausted by Shawn's same despondent attitude.

Shawn held a straight face and paused as if to decide whether he would go down the stairs or not. Everyone stared in his direction and the room was silent.

Rachel spoke up first. She felt the silence would make Shawn more uncomfortable. "Your brother talks about you all the time. You two must be very close," Rachel mentioned, as Shawn headed down the steps. "I'm glad I finally get to meet you," she continued, smiling as he finally reached the bottom of the steps. He gave no expression or reply to her, he just stood in front of her with his hands in his front pockets.

"This is Rachel, my beautiful bride," Tanner smiled proudly, hoping his brother would soon show the proper manners they were taught growing up and do something to return Rachel's greeting so as not to embarrass her.

"Nice to meet you," Shawn replied, bringing a smile of relief to Tanner's face. His voice remained monotone and the dark lines under his eyes revealed his stress and inner feelings. Tanner was proud of his efforts to be polite even though it was clear he was depressed.

"Hey, give your big brother a hug. It feels like I haven't seen you in forever." Tanner released Rachel and pulled Shawn into a big bear hug, lifting him off the ground. Shawn was as tall and nearly as broad as Tanner, but Tanner lifted him off the ground like he was a young boy. It actually made Shawn let out with a little chuckle, knowing it couldn't have been easy for Tanner to do. That little chuckle showed Rachel that Shawn had an inner fondness for his big brother all right. It was a tiny glimpse of how they must have goofed off together growing up.

"He's as tall as you are Tanner," Neil too had felt a spark of life when he heard his son chuckle. All three of the men in Tanner's family were handsome, strong and tall. The only difference with Shawn was he looked worn out and thinner. It was clear his phobias were affecting his health. Possibly exhaustion from lack of sleep and no appetite. Rachel knew firsthand how phobias could deprive you of your sleep and any desire to eat.

"So, you say you can't drive. Is that right little brother?" Tanner asked after putting Shawn back down on the ground. Shawn gave an ever so slight shake of the head signaling no.

"Well, I beg to differ. You've been driving these work trucks and tractors all over this winery since you were small. All we have to do is teach you some of the legal rules and how to dodge all the crazy drivers and you'll have your license in no time. We can even work together to shine up my old car for you. It'll be fun," Tanner encouraged. He was already at work trying to get his brother out of that bedroom and having a life.

"I don't really have any reason to drive right now." Shawn abruptly shut down and headed back up the stairs. It was as if Tanner had brought up a subject that wasn't allowed. The sudden departure and quick desire Shawn had to get away from everyone was a shock.

"Honey, how about coming and eating lunch with all of us. It'll be ready in just a few minutes," his mother asked in a forced, overly cheerful voice, trying to encourage him to not continue up the stairs. She had hoped his big brother being home would be reason for him to make some changes. She knew how close they were. Rachel could see the desperation in Victoria and Neil's faces. It was clear they haven't been having any success with Shawn for quite some time.

"No thanks mom, I'm not hungry," he mumbled. No doubt he loved his mother, but it was also very clear he wanted nothing to do with being near any of them at the moment. He continued up the steps without even a glance back their direction.

Rachel saw the disappointment and worry on Tanner's face as well. She knew he felt that it was his fault that Shawn went back upstairs; he must have said something wrong. She didn't feel the situation was as bleak as they all seemed to feel. She'd been through some major depression herself when she lost her mother.

"You didn't say anything wrong, don't worry," Rachel whispered to Tanner and gave his hand a squeeze. "We just got here. Give it time."

After seeing Shawn, she felt she may have ways of helping him but she wasn't sure. She had concerns of her own. One, he was a teenager with strong emotions which could make things very hard. Two, would she have any chance of getting him to speak to her about his feelings or was he already too closed down in his own world of depression? Three, will he dare to listen to anything she might have to say? After all, she was a total stranger to him. Last of all, will his parents go along with her ideas? She had no clue how it was going to play out but after looking into Shawn's dark eyes and seeing the worry on all of their faces, she needed to try.

***

Tanner and Rachel went upstairs to unpack. Their room was just a little way down the hall from Shawn's room. Rachel listened for music or game noises coming from his room but heard nothing. If he was playing games or watching videos, he made sure he used earphones so no one knew.

"He's got it bad," Tanner whispered as he emptied his suitcase, putting most of his clothes into the dresser drawers.

"Don't worry, Tanner. We just got here. Give it some time," she repeated. She moved over by him, then rubbed her hand up and down his back to comfort him. "He came down the steps, didn't he?" she continued. "That's a good start. Then he laughed when you picked him up. That shows he still connects with you on some level. Way down inside that depressed body is a guy wanting to come out and be happy. That gives me a lot of hope for him."

"That's true, he did laugh when I hugged him. That was unexpected." He reached out, pulling her into his arms and kissing her. His lips were warm and his touch was gentle. She loved kissing him and he loved how she always knew what to say to cheer him up.

"Look at this bed!" Rachel gestured towards the bed, trying to change the subject. The bed was king-size with a thick, white, fluffy comforter covering it. Rachel could just hear it calling her name as she glanced back at Tanner. Tanner gave her a tempting grin and off she ran, jumping in the air as she flipped over onto her back and landed in a large white cloud of softness.

"Oh my gosh," she moaned in sheer pleasure. "I feel like I'm floating." She spread her arms out and slid them up and down.

"It's called goose down," Tanner told her, laughing at her playful side.

As she continued to melt into the comforter, Tanner moseyed over to join her. He laid on the bed next to her and wrapped his arms around her. Pulling her close, he gave her a passionate kiss. He was happy. He had grown up in this room and now he was here with his wife. It felt good. No, it felt great.

It felt great to Rachel too. Being in his arms always felt good to her and to top it off, being in his amazing home was like being on another vacation.

Rachel could tell the room had to have been remodeled since Tanner was young, but she enjoyed the little remnants of his youth she noticed in the room. One of the walls in his room had a shelf with special edition model cars, one being a mustang which was no surprise to Rachel. On the top of both his dressers were miniature architecture buildings which he must have spent quite some time on in his teens. They were all done very well and it helped her see another side of Tanner: his younger years. She felt good knowing she was going to learn a lot about the man she married living here temporarily.

"I thought I'd keep you from floating away," he teased, wiping the loose hair from her eyes as he peered into them.

"Oh, did you now?" she smiled, knowing where this was leading. "Tanner," she warned, "we better get downstairs. Your mom is waiting for us. She made lunch. I don't want to get on her bad side on our first day."

His eyebrow lifted as he was deciding whether to argue the point. "Okay wife, you're the boss," he teased as he stood up.

"Very funny," she said, leaping up. She would have rather stayed in bed with him all morning if it were her decision, but she really did want to make a good first impression. They were going to be living there for a while and she didn't want her new in-laws thinking right off that she took anything for granted.

"Goose down, huh?" she peered one last time at the comforter, as if dreaming of its use later. "I want one of these for our bed when we get a house of our own."

"Absolutely." He smiled in agreement as she took his hand and encouraged him out of the bedroom with her.

Once in the kitchen, Rachel went over to the counter where Victoria had arranged a platter of sandwich makings and some salads. Rachel prepared plates for Tanner and herself and brought them over to the table. Victoria started to do the same for Neil and herself when Neil abruptly stood up, taking his plate from her and making his own. Rachel wasn't sure if he was trying to be helpful or if he was upset with Victoria. Feeling uncomfortable, Rachel acted like she didn't notice and asked about Shawn.

"Was there something that happened that originally set Shawn off into these attacks?" There was no response. For a moment, it was as if she hadn't even spoken.

Neil and Victoria went back to the table with their plates. When Victoria sat down, she nearly spilled her drink. When she grabbed for it, preventing the spill, Rachel could see that her hand was shaking. The table went silent for a moment, then Neil spoke up.

"We don't know for sure what caused it but we suspect it relates to when he lost two of his friends in a car accident a year ago," he looked at Victoria, annoyed, as he answered.

Rachel and Tanner's eyes met briefly. They both felt that the loss of Shawn's friends in death could definitely be a big part of what started his attacks.

They could also see that this wasn't the time to get in a discussion about Shawn. His parents were definitely stressed out. Quickly, Tanner changed the subject onto their honeymoon trip in hopes to get their minds on something more positive.

They discussed their two weeks in Kauai. Rachel talked about the beauty of the island and the wonderful foods whereas Tanner brought up all the funny experiences they had as they went snorkeling and sailing together.

"It took Rachel two hours to get fitted in the right mask that she would trust to snorkel with after reading all the negative comments online about the wrong-size masks. Once she went in the water with all the gear on, she felt claustrophobic and it took two more hours to actually get her snorkeling," he said with a laugh. Tanner knew Rachel found it funny as well because they had joked about it on the plane or he would have never teased her about it. He would never want to make her feel belittled. They both just chalked up the incident as part of the fun and experience.

"Tanner, you shouldn't tease her about that," Victoria said, feeling bad for Rachel.

"Oh, it's okay Victoria, because I have something to tease him about," Rachel countered.

"Rachel..." Tanner gave her a lifted eyebrow of warning.

"I'd like to hear it," Neil encouraged with a growing smile.

Rachel gave Tanner an evil grin, then went on, "Well, you know how the people of the island love Polynesian dancing and the hula?" She continued to smile at Tanner as she spoke, then turned her eyes to Victoria and Neil.

"Yes," Neil agreed, all smiles, knowing where this was headed.

"Put it this way, you should see Tanner in a hula skirt," Rachel started busting up as she looked back at Tanner's embarrassed face.

"A hula skirt?" His dad laughed loudly. "I would have loved to have seen that!"

"Oh, I can help with that," Rachel pulled out her phone and Tanner grabbed it out of her hand.

"Let's not show them everything just yet," he held it in the air out of her reach. "I have to work with this man you know."

Everyone laughed and Rachel skillfully changed the subject onto sailing so as not to embarrass Tanner too much.

"Our sailing trip was an experience," she explained. "I fell overboard right off. Tanner was trying to teach me how to sail and the waves would splash up on the boat making it slippery. I'd scurry around quickly trying to show Tanner I could be a great sailor but once when he gave me directions I slid right off the boat and into the water." She laughed, then added, "But that wasn't all; I accidently knocked Tanner overboard when I hit him with the boom. I think that's what you call it?" She looked at Tanner and he gave her a nod. "Sailing has its own vocabulary you know," she explained. "I think I'd have to take a whole semester in college if I wanted to learn it."

Neil and Victoria both knew what she was talking about because they were people who sailed. They had taught their boys to sail from a young age. Yet, at that moment, it seemed to Rachel that they were trying to avoid that good memory. As if not wanting to admit they did it together. Rachel just continued her stories knowing Tanner was already worried enough about his brother, she didn't want any other worries coming his way.

"At one point we both ended up falling overboard when the boat keeled over too far." She looked at Tanner again in hopes that she pronounced the word correctly.

"Rachel didn't quite understand the winds versus the waves when she was steering the boat and over we went. It was a fun experience, or should I say funny? Both words applied." Tanner gave a chuckle as he gave Rachel's hand a little squeeze.

"The boat had so many ropes all over it and you had to move and do different things with each one, it was crazy," Rachel looked at Victoria with exaggerated confusion.

"I felt the same way when Neil first taught me," Victoria agreed. "I never thought I'd learn it."

"But you did." Neil bluntly ended Victoria's trip down memory lane.

Tanner picked up on the bad attitude and spoke up, trying to cover up for his father's rudeness. "Rachel did a great job after we were out there for a couple hours. She just had to get the hang of it."

"That's true, once I got a grip and we both quit laughing and falling out of the boat," she added with a giggle, "then I did pretty good. We had a great time together that day."

Overall, Tanner's parents seemed to enjoy the stories and the lunch with Tanner and Rachel. It was good having their oldest son home again and they could tell they were going to love having Rachel around. Things had been pretty glum around their home the past year and they desperately needed some cheering up.

After lunch, Rachel and Victoria worked together cleaning up the kitchen and putting away the leftovers while Neil and Tanner sat discussing work. Rachel enjoyed helping with the cleaning; it made her feel like family. She was surprised Victoria did all the cooking and they didn't have a hired cook with the size of their home. It was

21

obvious they had the money for one. She planned to question Tanner later on that subject.

Rachel made a plate of food and set it aside until they were all done cleaning. It was a roast beef sandwich with about every delicious trimming you can put on it. There was also potato salad, fruit salad and two brownies.

"Still hungry?" Victoria asked, confused, when Rachel dished out the plate.

"Are you kidding, I couldn't possibly eat this much," Rachel laughed. "I'm taking it to Shawn."

The room got silent as all eyes turned in her direction. They looked like deer, caught in a car's headlights. *What's the big deal?* she wondered.

Chapter 2

"That's a sweet thought but he won't take it. We've tried. He won't even answer the door most of the time," Victoria divulged as she fought back tears. It was bad enough that he wasn't coming out of his room anymore but now he had stopped eating too.

"That's okay, Victoria," Rachel replied. She was holding the plate with one hand and squeezing Victoria's hand lightly with her other hand, a comforting gesture she picked up from Tanner. "It's just a connection I'm after right now. It doesn't matter if he doesn't eat it. He needs me just to offer it. He doesn't know me at all. Any little nice thing I do can help him start to trust me and that's important."

"You've got some help now, Mom, let her try," Tanner encouraged. He was actually trying to comfort his mother, knowing she was overwhelmed in her efforts to help Shawn. Neil and Victoria both forced a smile at Tanner's comment, desperate for any help they could get. Victoria felt if Tanner trusted Rachel to help her son then so did she. Whatever Rachel had planned, she would back up. It took a very special woman to win her son's heart over to the point of marriage and Rachel did. She had to be someone unique.

They were relieved to have help and to have some hope again. Neither one of them had much confidence, though, that anyone or anything could help. They were at a loss what to do; their son was not only losing weight quickly, but also losing himself. He was no longer the Shawn they once knew, full of life and smiles.

Victoria was worn out. She had tried everything she could think of as a mother to help her son and nothing was working. She tried babying him, tried to get him to vent and just talk to her, she tried gifts like video games or movies to take his mind off his extreme fears, special meals in hopes he'd get his appetite back, and even new clothes. Nothing worked, he rejected it all.

Neil on the other hand, just felt like he was letting his son and wife down. He tried to encourage Shawn with love, patience, different projects and even with doctors, but Shawn wouldn't have any of it. He even tried to get him to go on a trip with him just to get him away, but Shawn wouldn't go. Shawn just wanted to be left alone in his room. The deeper Shawn fell into depression the more Victoria told Neil that he needed to think of a way to help their son. Neil tried everything he could think of and yet couldn't succeed. He felt like a failure and had started to become bitter himself.

After a round of hugs, Tanner and Rachel went upstairs. Tanner waited by the door of their bedroom as he watched Rachel go down the hall to Shawn's door. He figured she had some sort of plan so he'd stay out of the way and let her do her thing.

"Shawn, it's Rachel," she said, knocking on his door. At first there was no reply, so she knocked again. "Shawn?" she paused, listening at the door for a response.

"Yeah," he finally answered but didn't open the door.

"I brought you some lunch in case you're hungry."

"No thanks," came the muffled reply. She was thrilled that he even spoke to her, being a perfect stranger and all.

"No problem, you don't have to eat it if you don't want to. I'll just leave it right outside your door in case you get hungry later." She listened for a response but there was none. "There's a delicious roast beef sandwich with about every trimming you can put on it along with some yummy sides and dessert. I figure if you're anything like Tanner you probably have a big appetite."

There was still no sound, but she felt that was better than him telling her not to leave it. She covered it with a napkin and went to the bedroom door where Tanner was waiting. She gave him a confident smile as she walked up to him.

"Have I told you how much I love you lately?" he asked. He loved how she was already focused on helping his brother and even showing concern for his parent's feelings.

"Not in the last few minutes," she teased with an amused smile, pushing him backwards into their bedroom.

"You really made my parents happy, knowing they have some help with Shawn," Tanner added, as he wrapped his arms around her waist.

"I hope I can make a difference, but it's really up to him and all of us working together," she explained, not wanting to let anyone down.

"I agree. Any change you help him to make is great, we don't expect miracles from you," he assured her. "As you can tell, it's really taking a toll on my parents. I'm worried about them." He dropped his hands off of Rachel and backed away slightly, showing something was on his mind.

Rachel was disappointed. She was hoping Tanner wasn't catching on to all of his parent's divisions, but he had. She knew it would weigh on him.

"I don't blame you for being worried, Tanner. They've been through a lot lately, but they'll work through it," she took a step towards him to reach out and comfort him.

"It's more than that," he started to say as he turned away, wandering towards the window. He wasn't able to look in her eyes as he spoke.

"What do you mean?" She knew something big was bothering him when pulled away from her again.

"My parents have always been a special couple. Throughout my whole childhood I've admired and wanted to be like them when I got married. All I've ever seen from them is deep love and respect for one another. Even through trials they've never wavered, they've always worked together through anything thrown at them." He pulled open part of the curtain to peer out the window as if he were looking for someone.

"I can see that in their marriage, it's very visible that they have strong love for one another. I hope we can always be like that. It's very rare these days." Rachel said, thinking back to their wedding, when Neil and Victoria acted like two love birds the whole day and night. She took a couple of steps towards Tanner, then paused, waiting for him to reveal his worries.

He turned his head to look at her as he held the curtain open. "Something is wrong," he said, firmly.

She backed away at his serious tone and took a seat at the end of the bed while giving him her full attention. She had never seen him this bothered before except for just before they got engaged when he thought he might be losing her.

"I can feel the tension between them," he peered back out the window. It was easier to reveal his thoughts if he wasn't looking directly at her. "Dad not letting my mom fix his plate for dinner? That's like a sin to her. Plus, she nearly spilled her drink when we brought up Shawn's name and did you see that her hands were shaking? Not to mention my dad cutting her off when she said he taught her how to sail." He dropped the curtain then turned and looked directly at Rachel, waiting for her response.

"Yes, I noticed that, but it's to be expected for them to have tension after all the pressure they've been under with Shawn for a whole year," she explained.

"I agree, but my father never gets short with my mother like this. He normally kisses her every time he leaves to go outside to work. Then, when he comes back from work, he normally pulls her close to him, happy to be back near her. She's like a precious gem to him. But he's not acting like that now. He's acting like a total stranger to her."

Rachel could tell Tanner felt like his whole family was falling apart and the fear of it was overwhelming.

"Tanner, I've seen him hold Victoria and compliment her since we've been here," she reasoned.

"Hardly. It's not the same. It's as if they're putting on a show to cover up their real feelings."

Rachel was silent as she thought about what Tanner was saying and what he really meant. *I can understand the shock and worry he's having if his parents rarely, if ever, fought growing up, but he seems even more worried than that. Could it be he's feeling that if their perfect marriage can't last, then maybe ours won't?*

"They probably are trying to cover up what is going on. They don't want their kids to worry about them splitting up. Also, they probably don't want everyone knowing their business. A year like they've had with their teenage son can cause tension in any person's marriage. But that doesn't mean they don't love each other anymore. It just means they're stressed." Rachel stood up, walking over to Tanner and gently taking his arm. "Tanner, you're not looking at this objectively. Take a step back and don't picture them being your parents, then I'm sure you'll realize they're just stressed out, not breaking up. Think about the love they clearly showed for one another at our wedding when they were dancing together. Do you really think all of that just left? Or maybe they're just showing signs of being two really stressed out parents right now?"

Tanner paused, thinking about what she said. He then looked down into her eyes again as he tried to think more objectively. A smile slowly crossed his face as he put his arms around her. "You're right. I don't know what's wrong with me, I'm acting crazy." He gave her a gentle kiss.

"No, you're not. You're acting like someone who cares about his family and you just need to give it some time for the situation to work itself out." She gave him a kiss this time. One with more passion. He gently backed her up until both of them fell together onto the bed letting out with a slight laugh. He was ready to forget his worries and focus on her and she was ready to help him with that plan.

An hour later, Tanner came down from their room and headed outside for his rental car. Rachel was just doing some finishing touches on her makeup and would follow. They had plans to go buy a new car today and to return the rental car to the airport. They didn't want to waste money on having a rental when Tanner's job wasn't paying for it anymore. They were also anxious to buy their first car together as husband and wife. They had already discussed what kind they wanted while they were on the plane coming home from Kauai. They had decided on a Toyota Camry. They felt it would be a good family car yet stylish at the same time.

As Tanner passed his father's office, the door had been left slightly open and he could see in. Neil was sitting, slouched over in his chair with his hands holding up his forehead. His father looked completely worn out and crushed. Tanner wasn't sure if it was due to Shawn's problems, his relationship with his mother, or both, but Tanner could tell it was bad. He knew his father well enough to know better than to reveal his presence there. His father is a very loving man to his family but very private with his own feelings. Tanner quietly continued to his car. When Rachel came down, he filled her in on what he saw.

Four hours went by before they arrived back home with their new car. It was a blue and sporty looking Camry. Tanner was in a hurry to see if he could get Shawn to come downstairs and go for a ride. Anything to get him out of the house.

"Shawn, come check out our new car!" Tanner yelled, looking upstairs to where Shawn would appear if he were to come out of his room. He knew Shawn could hear him, they had spent their whole childhood yelling back and forth to one another up those stairs.

Victoria came out of the kitchen where she had been preparing dinner for everyone. "He hasn't come out of his room since you arrived earlier," she warned Tanner.

Tanner ran up the stairs, skipping two steps at a time, and knocked on his door. He was eager for Shawn to come out. The food was still on the ground, covered and untouched. Tanner felt disappointment when he saw that his brother hadn't eaten, but he didn't give up.

"Hey, Shawn did you hear me? I got a new car. I want you to come check it out."

Nothing. No sound. Tanner waited. Still nothing. "Hey bro, did you hear me?" Still nothing. He was starting to get very concerned when the door handle finally turned and the door opened. Shawn stood there with a blank expression, staring at Tanner. His dark room and dark clothes were very worrisome to Tanner, but he tried not to show it. This wasn't the outgoing, happy, athletic brother he knew growing up.

"Come on, I think you'll love the color," Tanner said, trying to keep an upbeat attitude and hoping it would rub off on Shawn. Tanner headed down the hallway to the stairs as Shawn slowly followed. "We had to buy a car and quit using rental cars now that I'm not traveling anymore. I have to foot the bill most of the time instead of my job paying so I figured we need our own wheels." Tanner tried to keep talking in hopes that Shawn would keep walking and not turn around and go back to his room. They headed down the steps and Shawn slowed down with each step. The thought of going outside was like a nightmare to him.

Rachel had waited for Tanner and Shawn next to the front door. She felt sure that Shawn wasn't going to go outside to look at their new car but she hoped she was wrong. She knew Tanner would be very disappointed if he didn't.

Victoria stepped over by the couch, wanting to watch but not let Shawn see her.

Tanner didn't really care about showing off the car, but he did care about getting his brother out of the house and out of his depression. Tanner got to the front door, pulling it open nice and wide. He was proud to show off his new car to his brother. What he didn't realize was that all Shawn saw was the bright sunlight that came through the wide-open door and it was screaming danger to him. Not only did it make him stop in his tracks, but he instantly began to back step up the stairs.

"Where are you going?" Tanner asked, shaken by Shawn's reaction. "Come look at my car. It's just right outside the door here. You don't have to go far."

Shawn turned one last time, trying to acknowledge his brother before he got to the top of the steps. He was glad his brother was home; he just couldn't chance anything bringing on one of his attacks. Going anywhere outside would bring one on for sure. He couldn't explain that to Tanner because he was afraid that talking about them would also bring one on.

Tanner stared up at Shawn, helpless and confused. Shawn looked at him, then at the wide-open front door once more. His body began to sweat. Panic filled his face and he became pale. Just the tiniest thought of going outside sent him into a troubled state.

"Tanner, wait!" Rachel whispered. Touching his hand to gently silence him, she turned her attention to Shawn. "Shawn, don't worry, you don't have to go outside. It's okay," she assured him in a calm voice. Turning to Tanner once more she whispered, "Close the door most of the way." Tanner did as she suggested and slowly closed the door most of the way.

Shawn liked that the door was starting to close.

"I don't-" he started to say, as he stared at Rachel.

Rachel interrupted him, "I know. You don't have to," she replied quickly. Shawn figured she was saying he didn't have to look at the car, so he turned to continue walking up the stairs to head for his room. Rachel stopped him.

"I have an idea Shawn," she encouraged, and he stopped to listen to what she had to say.

"I've had the same feelings in the past as you're having right now and I found ways around them. Ways to make it so I could do the things I wanted to do. Ways without having a panic attack," she encouraged.

Shawn turned his head to listen to her but not his body. He was surprised she actually knew he was having panic attacks. It was obvious to all, but she actually said the words out loud. Plus, she admitted that she's had them herself. This interested him. She had his attention now.

"For instance, this car. I think you want to see it but you're worried about having an attack. When I used to have that happen, I'd take tiny steps. That means don't go out the door. Don't even think about going out the door, it's out of the question. Just try to walk to the door and look out at the car. That would be a big step. You get to see the car which is something I think you want to do but also not go outside where you feel you'd have a panic attack. Don't let these feelings control your life, Shawn. Take your life back. Do something you want to do."

He slowly turned around and stared at her, taking it all in. He was shocked she was talking to him like this, yet he felt desperate for help from someone who might actually know how he's feeling. The whole room was silent and no one moved. They couldn't believe he had even stayed that long as she spoke to him.

She could see the turmoil on his face. It was obvious he hated being trapped the way he was inside his uncontrolled mind. He continued to stare, not moving from his position. Rachel could tell it was really causing him stress trying to decide what to do, so she had to make another move.

"We'll leave the door just like it is and not open it any farther. You can just take your time, there's no hurry. You just look out the door, see the car, and you're done. You don't even have to stand in front of the door opening if you don't want. You can stand behind the door and peer around it if you feel better doing that and we'll all understand," she suggested.

Tanner gave a slight smile to Shawn as if to agree with what Rachel was suggesting. He stayed quiet, not wanting to say anything that could scare Shawn back to his room.

Shawn slowly started walking down the steps once more. He stopped just before the landing, staring at the front door.

"That's it, you're doing great. Take your time. You can come over next to me to start with if it makes you more comfortable," she suggested, signaling by her side which was about three feet away from the front door.

It was clear that Shawn's mind was ticking away at a hundred miles an hour as he tried to decide his next move. He seemed extremely cautious, but it wasn't the people he feared. It was that dreaded attack he felt might get set off from any wrong move he made. They weren't your average panic attacks.

He made it down the last two steps, not taking his eyes off Rachel. He wanted to avoid that front door. It was only slightly open, but it may as well have been all the way open to him. He stepped over closer to Rachel, turning his eyes to the floor. He paused there, terrified yet almost relieved, as if her presence created a safe zone, as long as he didn't move.

"Nothing is going to happen, you're just looking out the door at the car, that's all. You're not going out there," Rachel assured him. For some reason he already had some trust building up in her. Rachel figured the combination of being Tanner's wife (whom Shawn looked up to) and saying she's had these feelings herself before might be why. Whatever the reason, she hoped he'd keep trusting her.

He looked at her briefly once more, then at the door, and took a step towards it.

"Good, you're nearly there, you're doing great," she said in a calm, steady voice.

He took two more steps and was there in front of the partially opened door. He looked out at the car then quickly moved back to the stairway.

Tanner wondered if he even got to see the car, it happened so quickly. Rachel acted nonchalant and said, "Well, what do you think of the color, Shawn?" She didn't want Shawn to feel stupid for how quickly he had looked or for any of his reactions. He had taken a big step just now and she wanted to acknowledge it.

"Cool," he said with a shaky but happy tone. He knew he had accomplished something big for him. It was hard for him to remember the last time he even looked out the door. His first step was over and he quickly headed back up the stairs before anything bad could happen.

"Nice job, Shawn," Tanner yelled to him as Shawn disappeared back into his room.

Rachel looked at Tanner and they both smiled. Victoria hurried over to Rachel from where she had stayed out of view. She was very happy and was about to say so when Tanner put his finger over his lips then pointed for them all to go into the kitchen where they could all talk freely. Once there, Victoria couldn't control her excitement.

"You're so good with him I can't believe it," Victoria said, giving Rachel a big hug.

"Your son has been just as good with me many times," Rachel explained, thinking about Tanner and the gentleness and patience he had shown her anytime she's been afraid.

"But somehow it's harder for me with my brother. I know what he used to be like, and I think I push him sometimes instead of being more patient," Tanner admitted.

"He hasn't even looked out that door in months," Victoria stated. She glanced out the kitchen window as if to make sure Neil wasn't around, then took a seat at the kitchen table. Tanner and Rachel sat down as well, sensing that she had something startling to tell them.

Chapter 3

"I just want you both to know what you're dealing with when it comes to Shawn," she started to explain. Tanner and Rachel nodded their heads in agreement for her to carry on.

"He was so desperate for help about three months ago that we managed to talk him into going with us to another psychiatrist. Some of our friends told us there was a really good one here in town."

"He actually went outside?" Tanner was amazed.

"Yes, he wrapped himself up in a long trench coat with a hood and covered his face, feeling it would prevent his attack. We guided him holding his arm and directing him into the car and into the psychiatrist's office. He was only in the room with the psychiatrist for maybe five minutes before he ran out of the office and out of the building completely. We could see his color was off and we knew he must be having one of his attacks. The psychiatrist came out of his office right after Shawn with great concern on his face. Your father immediately took off after Shawn." Her hands began to shake as she went on with her story. Tanner took her hands and held them, trying to give her comfort as she continued.

"Shawn ran right out into the busy street without hesitation." Tears filled her eyes as she recalled that fearful day.

"Oh my," Rachel's hand went up over her mouth.

"What?" Tanner was shocked.

"I don't think it was just because he was running from the panic attack. I think it was because he was giving up on life," her nose started to drip as she began crying.

Rachel quickly retrieved a couple of napkins knowing she'd need them.

"Vehicles were slamming on their brakes and skidding everywhere. People were yelling and honking. I'd never been that scared in all my life. Your father ran and caught up to him. He wrapped his arms around him tightly, lifted him off the ground, and carried him out of the road. Shawn fought and kicked to get away at first, but Neil wouldn't let go."

Tears poured down her face as she recalled the horrible event. "His fighting didn't last long because he was having too much trouble breathing with his panic attack and just begged us to bring him home. We could hear him crying underneath his trench coat as we drove, but he wouldn't let us comfort him. He didn't want anyone to speak to him or touch him." She continued to cry, letting out her grief.

Tanner and Rachel were distraught by what they heard. Victoria went on, wanting so much for Tanner to know what they've been going through and hoping for some type of good advice.

"We were just beside ourselves after we got home. We thought our stress and worries couldn't possibly get any worse until we got a knock at the door. Some people came, checking to see if Shawn needed to be under suicide watch.

Of course, the psychiatrist had called them, afraid that Shawn was trying to kill himself," Victoria continued.

"I'm not surprised. I would think it's his job to do that. What did you do?" Rachel asked, with concern.

"Shawn convinced them when he was questioned that he wasn't trying to kill himself, he was just frightened and running from the panic attack," Victoria explained. Tanner looked relieved until she added, "But we knew the truth."

"Shawn promised the people he'd take some antidepressant medicines from the psychiatrist and they agreed not to take him away from his home. It was good he was still a minor or we'd have had no say at all." Her tears had slowed to a mild drip now as she continued with the rest of the story. "We had hoped the medicine might make a big change. We were happy when he finally agreed to take it."

"What happened when he took it?" Tanner questioned.

"He didn't give it long enough to even test it. After only taking a few, he claimed they weren't helping, all they were doing was making him sleepy. Then he stopped taking them."

"What's wrong with sleep? It looks like he could use some?" Rachel questioned.

"That was our thought too. He told us that when he took the medicine all he did was sleep and had a hard time staying awake at all."

"What did the people do when they found out he quit taking it?" Rachel questioned.

"Nothing. They don't know he's not taking it. Shawn convinced them the medicine was working and he had us refilling the prescription every thirty days to make it look like he was taking it. I know that was wrong for us to do, but we didn't want them to take him away from us. We figured that in his room at least he'd be safe and not hurt himself."

"Didn't they question you two as well?" Rachel wondered.

"When they questioned us, Neil and I backed Shawn up, afraid they would make things worse. I know that was probably the wrong thing to do and we probably made him worse because of it but we just didn't know what to do. We had never dealt with anything like this before. They told us they had so many teenagers with much more serious problems and living under horrible conditions that they had to help them too. Eventually, they stopped coming around," she confessed, then dropped her head in her hands, feeling like a failure.

Tanner's fist hit the table. "I should have been here; I had no idea it was this bad."

"No, Tanner," Victoria quickly lifted her head. She didn't need another one of her sons upset. "It wasn't your fault."

"Tanner," Rachel got his attention by touching his arm. "Your mom doesn't need you upset right now, she needs your strength and support, not your anger."

Tanner quickly calmed himself, knowing Rachel was right. His mom was overwhelmed already. He patted his mother's hand and told her everything was going to be all right.

"This is no one's fault, you two," Rachel spoke up. "The first thing everyone needs to do is to quit blaming yourselves. These things happen, you just have to deal with them. At this point we all need to just work together to help Shawn get better. I think I can help. It's going to be a really slow process," Rachel warned Victoria, knowing from her own experience that it doesn't happen overnight. Plus, she didn't want Victoria's hopes too high. She explained that she wasn't a doctor, but she was someone who could relate to what he was going through from her own experiences. She told her she knew different techniques that worked to help her and that she felt could possibly help Shawn as well.

"I can tell he wants to change," Rachel added to give Victoria and Tanner encouragement. "He pushed himself just now; that's a really good sign. He also grew some trust in me which is a big thing if I'm going to be able to help him in any way."

Victoria listened but her eyes focused on the window. All she cared about was that something different was happening in her son right now. It was small, but it was the first sign of change they'd seen in a long time and she liked it. "Neil will be happy to hear how you got him to look out the door and how you have ideas to help. I can't wait to tell him when he comes in for dinner." Victoria got up and stepped towards the window, peering out to see if she could spot her husband anywhere. She was grabbing on to any positive she could after a year filled with negatives.

Tanner squeezed Rachel's hands gently, giving her that special smile of his that was meant for her alone. He was thankful she was there and helping with this situation. It meant everything to him.

Neil didn't come in for another hour, but when he did, the four of them enjoyed a pleasant dinner. The mood was lifted because things were starting to change for the better. It was obvious to Tanner that when things were going well with Shawn, his father wasn't as short with his mother, but when he was worried, the tension was there.

After dinner, they moved into the spacious front room by the fireplace, each with a glass of wine. Victoria sat on the couch by Tanner and Rachel, not in the chair next to Neil. Tanner was realizing that his mother still has issues with his father, even though she still rushes to share good news with him.

Neil dimmed the lights, not showing that he had noticed, then he flipped a switch on the wall and the large stone fireplace lit up. The fire filled the room with colorful flames and flickering shadows. It was beautiful and relaxing. Rachel couldn't help but think of how Shawn must miss all of these pleasures.

They spent a long time talking about the winery and the harvest. Neil and Tanner explained to Rachel about the different color grapes and the type of wines each one made. Most of all, they explained how harvest time was coming soon and what that meant. Rachel learned quickly that harvest time was the biggest time of the year for winemakers. All their hard work leads up to the harvest. They have to pick the grapes precisely at the right time; it was very important. Not too soon or the grapes aren't sweet enough and not too late or the birds and bad weather would get them. It's a very serious yet exciting time of the year. It's also a fun and happy time of year for all involved. After the picking is done, they have a huge party to celebrate all their hard work throughout the past year.

"It sounds exciting! I'm glad we'll be here to be a part of it," Rachel said as she sat next to Tanner with his arm around her. She felt content as the soft leather couch gave way to their bodies. However, Rachel couldn't help but change the subject back to Shawn since she couldn't get her mind off him.

"When does he eat?" Rachel whispered to Victoria.

"Not often anymore. When he thinks everyone is sleeping, he'll come down sometimes to eat and hurry back upstairs. We can hear him. We don't come out of our room because if we do, he'll just hurry back to his room and not have anything to eat. He told us that being near people or coming downstairs could bring on an attack, so he avoids us like a plague. That's why we were shocked when he came downstairs to greet you and to see your car," she glanced in Neil's direction, as if expecting him to join in on the conversation, but all he did was look quickly away and stare at the floor, bothered.

"I'm going to bring him another plate of food," Rachel said as she stood up and headed back to the kitchen to make him a plate.

"He didn't eat the last one," Tanner commented, confused.

"That's okay, I'll bring him one every meal until he finally does," she voiced, determined. Tanner looked at his parents and they both smiled, admiring her determination and confidence.

Once Rachel had prepared a plate of food, she and Tanner went back upstairs. Rachel again left the food by the door after knocking and informing Shawn it was there.

"No worries if you don't want it, but just in case you get hungry, it's out here. There's some delicious lasagna your mom made. She's going to have to teach me how to make it for Tanner. I'm not the greatest cook. There's french bread and some awesome green beans with bacon. I love the way your mom puts bacon in the green beans, I've never had it that way before. There's also a slice of pumpkin pie. I hear it's your favorite. Anyway, it's right out here if you do get hungry. Have a good night Shawn, we'll see you tomorrow."

There was no response, but Rachel didn't care. No response was better than a bad response. She talked to him through the door as if they were having a normal conversation. She knew he needed to get involved with life and people again. She was determined to eventually get him curious as to what he was missing out on. He wasn't going to know that if people didn't tell him because all he sees is four walls. He needed to know life was worth fighting for and being locked up in his room wasn't a life.

***

The next morning, Tanner woke Rachel. He was already dressed and ready to start his day. "Rachel, I have a surprise for you," he whispered in her ear.

She forced one eye open as the sun beamed through the window, blinding her. She pulled her covers quickly over her head, dodging the light.

"You'll want to see this Rachel," Tanner tempted her, pulling at her blanket slightly. She rolled over to get the sun away from her face before opening her eyes once more.

"What is it you think I'll want to see?" she asked, curious, looking at Tanner and trying to adjust her eyes. He always had good surprises and she didn't want to miss out on any. He took her hand, carefully pulling her out of bed and to their bedroom door. Opening it quietly, he pointed toward Shawn's room. She peeked around the door and noticed his plate was clean of all food.

"He ate it!" she said with excitement. Tanner covered her mouth quickly, pulling her back inside the room and shutting the door before Shawn could hear her.

"I know. He didn't leave a crumb," Tanner said, pleased. "What do you think that means?"

"I think that means he was hungry," she teased with a laugh, falling on the bed. She was in a great mood now, knowing they were already getting somewhere with Shawn.

"That's not what I meant," he laughed, grabbing a pillow and tossing it at her face. "I meant, does that mean he might want to try going for a drive with us in the new car to get out of the house?"

"No. There's no way he'd do that right now. Going outside is his biggest phobia. I do have an idea I want to try with him today if you didn't already have any plans for us. Maybe you can help your dad at the winery while I'll stay here and try to work on my plan."

"What kind of a plan?" Tanner asked, sitting on the bed next to her.

"One that won't include trying to make Shawn go outside. Don't forget that I told you all of this is going to take time, Tanner. There's no quick fix here," she warned, knowing Shawn's situation was complex.

"Well, so far you're the only one getting anywhere with him. I'll just follow your lead. I'll go work out in the vines with my dad today like you mentioned. I've been gone a long time and this being the harvest season, I'm sure he could use my help. You do your idea with Shawn and we'll get back together for lunch, does that sound good?" Tanner suggested.

"Sounds great." She gave him a kiss.

"For now, get dressed and come down to breakfast with your hungry husband. I know you, and you need your two cups of coffee in the morning before you're good to do anything," he gave her a quick grin and started to head for the door.

"Tanner?" She had been curious for a while now and had to ask.

"What?" he stopped.

"Your parents are pretty well off, I can't help but be curious as to why your mom doesn't have any hired help to do the cooking and cleaning around here?"

"When it comes to cooking, my mom loves to cook. That's her enjoyment in life besides her family. Have you noticed the stove she cooks on?"

"Yes, it's unbelievable."

"My dad ordered all the best appliances for her, knowing it's her hobby. As far as the cleaning, she doesn't like workers cleaning in her kitchen. She feels it's her job to cook for her family. The rest of the house is something different, she does have some help with that they just come on certain days."

"That just seems like a lot for her to do by herself, especially with us here," Rachel said, worried.

"I know. Dad worries too. He refuses to let her throw a party unless she lets the workers help her and he doesn't let her tell us no if we offer to help her clean.

"Your dad sounds like an awesome man." Rachel was impressed by the love he showed for his wife.

"As for the workers and the housework, you'll see them around but not often. They work quickly and are in and out before you know it. They like to try to stay out of the way. They're a really nice bunch of workers. Their names are Tony, Maria, Sam and Teresa; if you do see them, go ahead and introduce yourself. I'm sure my mom already told them about us being married. They love my mom because she's so good to all of them. She insists on cooking them treats every day. Which reminds me, if you have any dirty clothes, there is a laundry chute in the closet. Just drop the clothes in it and they'll have the clothes clean, pressed and back upstairs before the end of the day. They also clean the bathrooms and make the beds."

"I can do our room, they don't need to," she said, embarrassed.

"You don't want to take their jobs away, do you?"

"No, I just feel spoiled," she said, feeling uncomfortable. She felt like it should be her job to clean up after her husband and herself.

"I'll try to keep it that way," he said with a smile. He added, "You sound like my mom, the way you feel it's your job and not theirs. I like that." He was impressed with her as he left the room.

When they got downstairs and entered the kitchen, Neil and Victoria were already eating breakfast. The room was quiet and Tanner gave Rachel a cocked eyebrow as she headed for the coffee pot which told her it wasn't the norm for them to be this quiet.

Neil brought up work plans for the day, trying to cover up the friction between him and his wife. Tanner played along but Rachel felt the worry building in Tanner.

After breakfast, Rachel stayed to help Victoria clean up the dishes. Victoria wasn't saying anything at first, but Rachel could see the tension building up in her.

As Rachel prepared a plate of food for Shawn, she couldn't help but ask Victoria if she was okay.

Victoria broke down. She dropped her dish towel on the table, sat down, and tried to cover her face as she cried.

"Victoria, what is it?" Rachel quickly hurried over to comfort her. She sat down in the chair next to her and put her hand on her back, rubbing it.

"Nothing, I shouldn't act like this. This is the second time I've cried in front you. I'm really not like this, I promise." She tried to dry her eyes with the dish towel and fight back the tears. She straightened up in her chair, ashamed for her own actions. Rachel was nearly a stranger to her and here she was about to pour her heart out to her. She didn't care at this point. She needed another woman to talk to and Rachel seemed like a good one.

"Why not? You're human, you have a right to get upset just like the rest of us," Rachel assured her, wanting her to open up. She needed to let everything out. Apparently, she had been holding something else in for a while.

Victoria broke down, continuing to cry into the dish towel, exhausted from stress and worry. "I'm sorry, but Neil and I have been worried for such a long time over Shawn that I think I've lost Neil over it."

"Why do you think that? He always acts like he loves you."

"He's just covering up, not wanting to hurt the boys," she looked at Rachel through puffy, red, tear-filled eyes. "We've been having serious problems between us for months. Then, about three months ago, Neil and I had a fight and he stormed out, mad. He left in his truck and didn't come back for three days. I thought he'd never return."

"Shawn must have noticed that?" Rachel questioned.

"Shawn never knew because he hardly ever left his room. When he did, he scurried around briefly then hurried back to it, never wanting to be seen. He never knows anything that's going on around here," she cried, frustrated, as if she'd rather him see the fight then stay locked up in his room.

"But what about at our wedding? You two were like love birds! I can't believe that was all an act," Rachel countered.

"It wasn't. But just before we went to your wedding, Neil and I were fighting so badly that he started sleeping in the guest room. I didn't fight it, to be honest, because I've been irritated, not knowing where he went for those three days or who he might have been with. When the two of you arrived, he started sleeping back in our room for the sake of appearances." She wiped her eyes with the dish towel then continued. "It was great when we went to your wedding. I felt that old closeness Neil and I once had before all of this started," she smiled at Rachel remembering that day. "Until we came home and the stress was there once more," her face dropped and more tears followed.

"Don't you see, the love is still there. When you were away from all the problems, those feelings were still there, then when you came back to the stress, the friction came between you again. Most parents go through these same things any time there is a serious problem with one of their children. They love their children, it's just overwhelming when they feel they can't help them in any way. You haven't lost Neil. You've both simply lost track of your own lives temporarily. You've put them to the side. But you'll get them back. Shawn will get past this and you will build your relationship again. I can tell because every time he progresses in any manner, you two share it with one another and give each other affection, whether it's a kiss or hug," Rachel reasoned. She grabbed Victoria some tissue from the counter for her nose and returned quickly. Rachel was no therapist, but anyone could see what was going on with this relationship.

"I don't know. He's never been short with me to this degree in our whole marriage!"

"And you've probably never had this kind of concern where you can't even get a doctor that can help with your child. It has to be the worst fear a parent can have. Anyone would get short with their patience after a year of this. Haven't you gotten short with Neil at all during all of this?"

"Yes, I've done my share," she admitted.

"But you still clearly love him."

"Yes, I definitely do, he's my life," she had a gleam in her eye as the words spilled out.

"I'm sure you're still his too. Any time he is short with you, remember that it isn't you he's upset with, it's the stress he's feeling for your son. One day it will go away." Rachel gave her a confident smile.

Victoria felt relieved after getting to talk to another woman who can relate to her feelings. Everything Rachel had said made sense and she hoped that the stress with Shawn was all that was wrong with their relationship. She felt very grateful for this new daughter-in-law; someone she could talk to as a friend.

Once Victoria was feeling better, Rachel finished fixing Shawn's plate of food and prayed she was right.

"Well, here I go again," Rachel said with a confident look as she carried the tray of food past Victoria and headed out of the kitchen.

Victoria gave her a hopeful smile for her efforts.

Once upstairs, she knocked on the bedroom door.

"Hi Shawn, I brought you some blueberry pancakes, eggs and bacon." She felt as if naming off each item helped him picture the food and build his appetite. "I heard you like coffee. I have a nice hot cup of it here for you. You and I are going to get along just fine if you like coffee because I'm a coffee nut."

No sound came from the room.

"Shawn?" Rachel repeated lightly, starting to wonder if he might be asleep. By the dark rings under his eyes she figured he wasn't getting much sleep and she didn't want to wake him if he had finally fallen asleep.

Still no response.

"I'll just leave it right here for you." She spoke lightly once more, leaving the plate on the ground, covered with a napkin, then left to her bedroom.

Outside, Tanner had plans of his own to talk with his dad about his mother.

He had never done that before and was concerned how his father would react, but he had to try.

Chapter 4

Tanner found Neil sitting on a stool just outside one of the work sheds, coiling up some heavy rope. Tanner didn't know what he was planning to use it for, but he didn't care at the moment. He just wanted the opportunity to talk to his dad and right then looked like the perfect time. No one was around and it was just the two of them.

"Hey dad," Tanner came up behind him with a chipper voice.

"Hey son," Neil replied, not knowing if Tanner was just saying hello or if he needed something.

"I kind of wanted to talk to you about something personal," Tanner slightly stuttered.

Neil stopped coiling the rope to look up at Tanner's face. "What is it?"

"It's about you and mom," he blurted out before he backed out. Neil got quiet, as if thinking, then went back to his coiling. Tanner was quiet too, not knowing if he should continue.

"No need to go on, son," his dad spoke out, looking down towards his rope.

"What does that mean?" Tanner asked, confused.

"It means, I know where you're going with this discussion and there's no need. I'll take care of it," he told Tanner in a serious tone, looking up at him now. When Tanner was young and his dad ended an argument between him and his brother with that tone and look, it meant the discussion was over and he didn't want to hear another word. Tanner turned to walk away, feeling bothered, as if his dad was talking to him like a child not his adult son. That was, until Neil stopped coiling the rope again and spoke up once more.

"Thanks son, for helping me come to my senses."

Stunned, Tanner turned, looking in his direction. "I didn't even say anything!" Tanner replied, slightly irritated and confused.

"Seeing you and Rachel together makes me miss the closeness your mother and I had before this whole thing started with Shawn. I miss it. I know you see it. I'll fix it if she'll let me," he promised.

Respect and relief filled Tanner's heart as he gave his dad a smile and a nod, then changed the subject quickly. He knew it was the best thing to do while things were going smoothly.

"What are you planning to do with this rope anyway?"

"Honestly, I don't know. I just wove the rope together the past few days to relieve stress. My father used to do it when I was young. He said it helped to get rid of his tension." He looked at the rope in his hand, admiring the weave.

"You must be pretty stressed, that's an awfully long rope," Tanner teased, looking at its length.

"Yeah, I guess so." Neil lifted the rope, looked at it, and chuckled.

"Did it work?" Tanner couldn't help but question.

"It actually does," he glanced up at Tanner with a smile.

"Okay then," Tanner smiled back.

***

A half hour later, Rachel peeked out her bedroom door to see if Shawn had taken the plate of food and it had disappeared. It had to be in his room now and he had to be eating it. Thrilled with his progress, she shut her door quietly and waited for another half hour before coming out of her room. The empty dishes were placed back in front of his door on the floor.

"Shawn?" she knocked at his door. "Tanner is working with your dad today and I'm really bored. Will you play a game of checkers with me?" She paused, holding the checkerboard as she waited. She heard no response.

"We can do it in your room, you don't have to come out," she waited, and waited, but nothing. Ten minutes went by as she stood holding the game and waiting for a response.

"I'm still here, Shawn. I don't care if your room is messy. You can come to my room to play if you like," she continued, not giving up. A few more minutes passed as she stood at the doorway. "I'm still here," she reminded him. She figured the fact that he hadn't told her no or to go away meant something.

The door handle finally turned, and the door cracked open. Rachel felt a jolt of excitement.

She waited for Shawn to open the door further, but when he didn't, she slowly opened it herself. The room was dark except for the slight glow of light coming through the sheer curtains. Stepping slowly into the room, she could still smell the aroma of his breakfast in the air. It was clear to her that most of his time was spent on his bed with his iPad where he was sitting now with it next to him. The room was large and clean which was surprising for a teenager in depression. She was relieved that he wasn't in the stage of depression where he wasn't cleaning himself or his room. She figured he must be cleaning his own room because he doesn't allow anyone else into it. She also figured he was probably smart enough to throw his dirty clothes down the laundry chute for the staff to clean and return to his door.

She noticed a small computer desk in his room, but the computer was missing. Shawn sat dressed in the same dark clothes as before. Next to his bed was a small end table with a lamp. "How about if I set up the checkerboard right here on this end table?" Rachel asked as she reached over to grab the chair from the computer desk. As she slid the chair out, she saw Shawn's breakfast and dinner in the trash can next to the desk. *He didn't eat his breakfast or his dinner after all. Why would he clean the plate and put it outside his door, pretending he did?* She moved the chair without hesitation, as if she didn't see the food in the trash. Her heart skipped a beat when she saw a razor blade also laying in the trash can. *Oh God, please tell me he isn't cutting himself.* She had heard about teenagers who get so depressed they cut themselves to feel pain. It was a combination of punishment to themselves and an opportunity to feel something. It was a very sad and distorted way of thinking.

Oh boy, if I tell Tanner this he will freak out and it will really cause a mess of things. Yet, if he is cutting himself not only can he get infections, but he might accidentally hit an artery and bleed out. The pressure was tremendous on her now, that was for sure.

Shawn watched Rachel without speaking as she set up the game, putting all the chips on the board. It was hard for her to concentrate after seeing the food and razor blade in the trash. She was also uncomfortable in the dark room.

"Do you care if I turn on this lamp to have a little light? That way we can see the checkerboard. I don't want you having any unfair advantage over me just because I can't see," she teased, hoping to lighten the tension in the room. He didn't smile but gave a nod that it was okay to turn the light on. She was a guest in his space, she wanted to be a respectful one.

Once the light was on, she noticed a small, square box on the corner of his computer desk. Clearly it was something important to him that was put aside yet kept close for his reach. Again, she said nothing about the item and just focused on the checkerboard.

The first game was quiet except for little questions Rachel asked about rules. Shawn only answered with nods, no words. He won the first game and Rachel teased that it was just beginner's luck, challenging him to another. Still not speaking, he gave the okay for another game.

While they were each setting up their chips for the second game, she glanced quickly around the room. It had no posters or pictures on the walls. The room seemed very plain. She didn't feel it had always been that way from the athlete Tanner described his brother to be. She figured he must have put everything in his closet so as not to remind him what he used to be like before his attacks. It probably felt like a jab every time he looked at them.

The second game wasn't as easy for him to win, but he still succeeded. Rachel now had her competitive streak going as they continued into another game. This time she won, leaping up from excitement. He wasn't an easy person to beat. Shawn couldn't help but give a little chuckle when she jumped with joy. She could tell he was starting to enjoy himself and relax. By the fourth game, he had joined in with some little sarcastic remarks of his own about her playing strategy. By the fifth game, Rachel tried to get conversations going by telling him how she and Tanner first met.

She started with what happened at the airport, how she was having panic attacks because she was terrified to fly and how Tanner would help calm her. Shawn got quiet and she could tell it disturbed him, talking about the panic attacks, but she carried on as if it didn't bother him. She knew he needed to hear some of it to be able to connect with her.

She told him how she nearly missed the flights. About how the airline attendant nearly took her carry-on away and how it made her have such bad panic attacks that she felt like she couldn't breathe and would pass out at any moment. She then explained how Tanner helped her through each situation.

Shawn wasn't that impressed until she brought up the situation with the drunk man sitting next to her and harassing her. She related how Tanner intervened and she felt sure that if the man hadn't moved when Tanner told him to, that Tanner would have moved him. Shawn was becoming very interested now, and it seemed to be relaxing him.

"Tanner called you his wife?" Shawn questioned with a laugh. "He didn't even know you."

Rachel spent four hours in Shawn's room, playing checkers and telling him stories. She told him all about how his brother gave up his first-class seat to her on the second plane just to help her not to be afraid of flying, while he had to sit at the back of the plane in coach.

"But it worked," she told him, content with the outcome.

"That's my crazy brother all right," he spoke out.

"The man on the plane followed me after the flight and attacked me one night. Your brother and his friend had to save my life, literally. They actually were on the pavement fighting it out with the guy." She knew a young man his age would love hearing the details. "Ron saved me and then Tanner saved him. They are a couple of Real Heroes."

Shawn beamed as he imagined his brother as the hero in these stories. He secretly hoped they'd never end.

It was clear that Shawn was a person who had been cooped up for a long time, bored, and now he had some excitement in his life again hearing these experiences. It was something interesting enough to overpower his thoughts of panic, at least for the moment.

"I also have a hot air balloon experience to tell you, where your brother fought an actual alligator," Rachel added enthusiastically.

"No way, I don't believe you. This has got to be all made up," he teased. It was energizing, like watching a superhero movie, and he couldn't believe it was all true. But it was. He knew his brother was always a strong and caring man, but he didn't expect this from him.

"I swear on my wedding ring that it's the truth and you know that's a big thing for a woman, especially a new bride. If you want to hear more, I'll come back tomorrow and tell you more. Would you like that?" she asked as she stood up from the bed and started putting all the checkers in the game box to leave.

"I'd like that," he admitted, feeling good for the first time in a very long time. "Can you come back tonight instead of tomorrow? I'd really enjoy hearing more of these stories." He was desperate to keep these good feelings coming. It was like being able to breathe after being short of breath for so long. She understood those feelings and didn't want to let him down.

"I promised Tanner I'd be with him later tonight, but how late are you awake?" She put the lid on the top of the game box and picked it up.

"I can't sleep at night. I hardly ever sleep," his voice got low as his eyes drifted away from her. He started to look depressed again, knowing the minute she left those bad feelings would return.

"Okay then, I'll come back at about 10:00 p.m. tonight. Tanner is usually asleep by then. He gets up super early before its light out to help your dad. I'll come back then, if you promise me one thing."

"What?" he asked warily as he turned to look at her.

"You actually eat the next meal I bring you," she said, glancing towards the trash can to let him know she was aware he'd been throwing his food away.

He paused to think about whether he could actually keep that promise before answering. "Okay, I promise," he agreed in a quiet tone.

She smiled, pleased.

"By the way," she added, "why didn't you just leave the tray with the food on it outside the door? You didn't eat the food. Why bring it in here just to throw it away?"

"You were trying to be nice, I didn't want to hurt your feelings. I don't eat because I'm not hungry. It's not to worry people. You won't believe how hard it is to get yourself to eat food when your body doesn't crave it at all," he told her honestly.

"Fair enough," Rachel accepted his honest answer.

"Bring the checkerboard," he suggested when she turned to leave the room. "You're one game ahead and I want to change that."

"You can try," she turned his way again, shooting back the dare. "Actually, I'll leave the checkerboard right here and you can plan your strategy until I come back later. You'll need it if you plan to beat me," she teased, placing the checkerboard back on the small table, then heading out the door.

He felt good, knowing she'd be coming back later. Better than he had in a long time. He enjoyed her company.

She couldn't believe she had been in his room for four hours. Tanner wasn't in their room and there was no sign of anyone else in the hallways or living room. She thought she'd better check the kitchen; Victoria is normally there. The minute she entered the door, Tanner, Neil and Victoria were looking at her with smiles on their faces. It was plain to see they must have been talking about Shawn.

"Dad and I just came in from the vineyard and mom told us you've been with Shawn all this time, talking and playing checkers. She said she could hear Shawn laughing and chatting away with you. I can't believe it," he said. He lifted her up off the ground and twirled her around, then gave her a big kiss.

"Neil, our son was having fun," Victoria brought out, delighted. She couldn't resist but give her husband a kiss on the lips, sharing the moment.

Tanner glanced at Rachel, giving her a slight grin, pleased with his parent's sign of affection and that his father didn't pull away this time.

Victoria then turned to Rachel. "Rachel, I'm sorry to snoop but I couldn't help it, I listened outside the bedroom door." Turning her attention back to her husband once more, she added, "I sat on the floor for hours just listening to our son joke with Rachel about the game and laugh at all her stories. He was having fun and he was happy," Victoria beamed. Neil looked like a weight had been lifted off his shoulders. A very serious weight. Joy covered his face and Tanner's as well.

That's when Rachel decided not to say anything about the razor blade. She thought to herself that if Shawn continued on an upward path, she wouldn't bring it up. This family didn't need more worries. She only prayed she was doing the right thing.

"You don't have to apologize, Victoria. This is your son and I'm a stranger to you. Anytime I'm with your son in his room or anywhere else, feel free to listen in and ask me any questions you please. I want to help the situation, not make more stress for you," Rachel told her sincerely.

"Thank you, Rachel, but I want you to know this: you're not making things stressful, you're making things better in ways you don't even know. Also, my son married you which means you're a pretty special woman, so I trust you completely," she confessed, giving her another hug.

"Thank you, Victoria, that means a lot," she hugged her back. "I'm glad to see Shawn like this, it makes me very happy. However, you guys all need to know this is still going to take a lot of time before he's better. He is going to have major ups and downs and you don't want to be shocked by it or it will set him back. He will have another panic attack, that I'm sure of, but don't be discouraged by it. It's going to take time and patience until he learns how to handle the attacks. One bad experience or wrong attitude from someone can set him back enormously."

They all listened carefully. They wanted Shawn to do well and Rachel had been the only one who had experienced these problems first-hand and the only one able to get through to him so far.

After dinner that night, Rachel brought a plate of food to Shawn. He actually opened the door when she knocked and took the tray of food. She reminded him of his promise. "No hiding it under your bed or in your closet," she teased. He gave a slight smirk, then a nod of agreement to her joke, knowing she was also serious. She left him with the tray and promised to return later after she spent some time with Tanner.

***

Later that night, Rachel and Tanner spent time walking around the winery. Rachel loved the colorful lights that lit up all the handrails and statues. They added to the winery's natural beauty and beamed like the stars above. Tanner had other thoughts on his mind. Rachel could tell by his expression that he was up to some scheme.

Tanner led Rachel to a quad that was parked near some grapevines and out of sight. He got on the quad and Rachel climbed on right behind him, putting her arms around his waist. He drove them up and down the rows of grapes until he stopped at a secluded spot in the orchard. There was a blanket already laid out on the ground with a very small lantern. It provided just enough light to see the two glasses of wine that had been poured. The moon was full, and the stars were bright for viewing.

"I thought we could use some alone time." Tanner gave her that flirtatious smile she loved. He put his hand out like a gentleman to help her off the quad.

"I couldn't agree more." Rachel gave him an enticing smile in return as she took his hand. "This is wonderful, Tanner."

Tanner sat down on the blanket and Rachel slid down right in front of him. He pulled her closer and she could feel heat shoot through her senses, and she knew he felt it as well.

"This is the life," Tanner said, letting out a happy moan. He was holding his new bride in his arms, surrounded by beautiful grapevines and ripe colorful grapes ready for the picking as far as the eye could see. The beauty surrounding them and the luminous full moon took their breath away.

She could feel the warmth of his cheek against her face as he held her close. He gave her neck a gentle kiss.

"It sure is," she agreed, as the warmth of his love filled her heart. She squeezed his arms to tighten his grip around her waist. She loved the feel of his strong arms holding her. It made her feel loved and secure; that was everything to her.

They slowly drank their wine, enjoying their time alone together. After twenty minutes, Tanner stood up and strolled over to the vines to check some of the grapes. Rachel followed out of curiosity.

"You know you are amazing with Shawn," he complimented her, but kept his back to her. She could see the grapes he was aimed for and they hung heavily, filled with juice.

"Thanks," she was slightly embarrassed and didn't know what else to say.

"How do you know so much about panic attacks?" He picked a grape from the bundle then turned to look at her, giving her his full attention.

"When my mother died, I began having panic attacks. As I got older, they got worse and worse. Beth insisted I see a therapist, but I was afraid and refused to go. Rebecca eventually got me to go. She actually went to a lot of my appointments with me otherwise I wouldn't have gone. I learned a lot through the therapy. I sympathize with what Shawn is going through and I know how to help him if he keeps letting me." She was ashamed to admit her past issues, but as her husband, he had a right to know.

"Well, if you're any example of how he can turn out, then he'll be great," he said with pride. Nothing she told him made him feel any less proud to have her as his wife. She loved helping people just like he did and he loved that about her. She showed that already when she left college to help her aunt in Florida for months after her uncle died. Now she was helping Shawn and swallowing her pride to do it.

"Thanks, Tanner," she said, feeling herself blush. She was relieved that he felt that way and even more relieved when he changed the subject away from her.

He tossed the grape he was holding into his mouth, tasting its readiness and flavor. "It won't be long now," he told her. "By the way, I talked to my father about my mom and I think things might start getting better between them. At least, I hope. My father told me he misses the closeness they used to have whenever he watches us together," he smiled proudly at her. "He's a little concerned my mom might not forgive him though, I don't know why."

"I do," she looked at the ground not knowing if she should say.

"What do you know?" His eyebrows narrowed.

She looked up at him innocently. "Your mom kind of let loose and vented to me early this morning. I think it was really good for her. However, she mentioned that your dad got mad a few months ago and took off for three days somewhere and she doesn't know where." Rachel was concerned about telling Tanner this, knowing it would be a big blow to him. His family just wasn't ever like this before.

"He did what?" Tanner was disturbed all right.

Rachel could see the hurt and confusion on his face.

"Your mom, like any woman, is concerned that he may have gone to another woman for comfort. I don't think he did, myself. He doesn't strike me as that kind of a man," Rachel quickly assured him. "But you can see why she might not be too quick to forgive him when he won't tell her where he went for those three days."

"No, I don't think he was with another woman either. He loves my mom, I know that," Tanner shook his head 'no' as he looked at the ground briefly, thinking. "But where he'd go for three days? I don't know. That's crazy. Everybody is losing their minds around here, I tell you." Tanner was overwhelmed. His family had changed so much and not in a good way, he just couldn't handle it.

"My parents and brother are acting like total strangers." He turned his face away from her, looking out towards the grapes and pausing to think. He was thinking back to the good times with his brother.

"My brother and I used to have such fun racing to see who could fill the most crates full of grapes during the harvest. It's hard to believe he won't be out here doing it with me this time." Tanner was feeling depressed. He reached out, feeling another clump of grapes in his hand, needing to fiddle. He tenderly rubbed them as if to feel their ripeness without breaking them.

Rachel had no clue how Shawn would be during the harvesting; it was too soon to tell. Likely, he wouldn't be out picking grapes. She'd be impressed if he'd just come out and see the grapes again, let alone pick them. As for his parents, if Shawn's health would get better, she had confidence the parent's problems would work themselves out.

"Tanner," she got up and walked over to him, putting her hand on his back and stroking it as she spoke. "Stress causes people to lose their minds and act like strangers. I have confidence that as Shawn gets better, and I feel he will, everyone will go back to being themselves again. This is rock bottom. There's nowhere else to go but up. Give it time."

He paused, thinking about her comments, then turned around slowly, forcing a small smile across his face.

The tightness of his smile told her he wasn't very convinced yet. She figured the best thing for her to do now was to change the subject and get his mind off his worries.

"I thought you'd have big machines that pick the grapes for you?" Rachel questioned. This winery seems to have all the same equipment she's seen on TV during harvest time. Surely, she figured, they'd have the same equipment here. A winery this big had to be up to date on that type of machinery.

"Yes, we do, but we have some large fields of grapes out there that have been here for many years. Those grapes make a lot of our special reserve wines. The problem is that they happen to be on a hillside where the harvesting machine can't safely go . Which means we have to pick all of those grapes by hand. We usually do it really early in the morning, at around 2:00 a.m. when it's still dark out. That way, the grapes don't get too hot once they're picked."

This was all very exciting to Rachel; she couldn't wait for the harvest.

That night, Tanner fell asleep by 10:00 p.m. as Rachel had predicted and she tiptoed over to Shawn's room, not wanting to alarm anyone in the household. She didn't know what Tanner would think about her staying up late at night to visit with Shawn, but she felt it was important. She knew Tanner trusted her, but she worried more about his parent's thoughts. They might not think it appropriate for her to be in a young man's room that late at night, and they would be right. But she had made progress with Shawn and she didn't want to chance losing the opportunity for it to continue.

Chapter 5

"Shawn," Rachel whispered outside his door. "Tanner's already asleep. Is it okay if I come in?" She knocked gently, trying not to wake other family members.

She could hear Shawn quickly come over and turn the knob to let her in. The light was already on in the room, showing Shawn's excitement for her arrival. That was a good sign, Rachel felt. Darkness always adds to depression. The sooner that habit stopped, the better off Shawn would be. The checkers were set up and ready to go and an empty tray of plates from his dinner sat on his computer table to prove he kept his word and ate his meal. Rachel saw it, then glanced in the empty garbage can and gave him a smile.

"Are you ready to lose to your sister-in-law again?" she teased.

"Wrong," he challenged back.

They played two games, each winning one.

"Rachel, tell me more about my brother and those adventures you had," he asked anxiously. It was obvious that his brother was his mentor.

She went on to tell him how Tanner stayed awake the whole night in front of her aunt's house in his car to make sure she was safe.

"That sounds like Tanner. He's watched out for me my whole life," he related with a chuckle.

"Who is this Ron guy? How'd Tanner know him?" Shawn inquired.

"That's another story," Rachel began. She went on to explain about Harvey's coffee shop where she met Ron and about the pet store flood.

"What started the fire?' Shawn wondered.

"Rats chewed a bunch of wiring in the attic causing a small fire and setting off the sprinklers."

"Oh, well that'll do it."

She went on to tell him about the loose snake in the water that rubbed against her leg and the tarantula that crawled across her hand, terrifying her.

"That's awesome," he said, thinking the whole situation was hilarious. "I would have loved to have been there while all that was happening."

"Thanks, you sound like your brother, all right," she replied with a smirk, "but I didn't think it was awesome at the time, that's for sure." Those comments just made Shawn laugh even more. Rachel smiled and continued on, knowing it was bringing enjoyment to Shawn.

"That was when your brother appeared behind me in the store, out of nowhere. No one even noticed him come into the pet store, we were all so busy. When I was throwing my hands in the air and freaking out from the spider, he came up behind me and put his hands on mine and gently pulled them to my side letting me know everything was all right. His warm hands and gentle touch made me feel so secure, I instantly forgot all about that dumb spider. I was thrilled to hear his voice again." She twirled her checker chip in her fingers, thinking about that day.

"Okay, let's not get me ill thinking about how my brother picked up on you," he teased.

Rachel laughed, then carried on telling him all about the hot air balloon ride and how Lily fell over the side and could have died but Ron and Tanner saved her. Next, she told him how they saved the pilot and fought off alligators.

"Are you telling the truth? They actually fought alligators? I still think you have to be making up these stories," Shawn was beside himself with disbelief.

"I swore on my wedding ring," she reminded him. "I promise you this is all true."

"Why couldn't I be a hero like my brother? I can't even go out of my room." Shawn couldn't help but get discouraged, even when he loved hearing the stories about his brother's strength and bravery. Tanner was a strong, confident man like his father, yet Shawn felt frail and scared. He hated that he wasn't like Tanner and yet they were all of the same blood.

"Shawn, it's all in how you look at things," she assured him.

"What do you mean?"

"I had similar phobias long ago. I even nearly drowned in the ocean. But I learned how to control my thoughts and overcame them and went right back into that ocean again. You can do it too. I didn't do it on my own, I had help. I had someone encouraging me about what to do and how not to give up. You have to help now too. We are your help."

His face showed doubt but the fact that he was questioning her showed he was thinking about it and wanting to change, which was hopeful.

She went on with her stories, not wanting him to get uncomfortable by talking too much about his problems. She wanted him to concentrate more on positive things, helping him just to feel some enjoyment at the moment.

She mentioned the little compliments Ron used to give her and it didn't take long for Shawn to figure out Ron had an interest in her.

"Sounds like Ron had a thing for you at the same time as Tanner," Shawn commented.

"Yeah, but he just kept getting stuck with Lily. His interest in me was put to a stop by Tanner the night Ron took me to his favorite club. That's when Tanner showed up and asked me to marry him. I thought I was going to die when he arrived at that bar and I was out with Ron," Rachel admitted as she fidgeted, stacking the checker chips in a tall pile.

"Why were you with Ron when you were already dating Tanner?" Shawn acted protective of his brother, as if she had been cheating on Tanner.

"Because…" she started to explain when all her chips fell, spreading across the small table making them both laugh.

Rachel explained to Shawn the whole reason she ended up out with Ron and why Tanner proposed that night at the bar.

"You're kidding, he was already mad because you were with Ron and when he tells you to leave with him, you told him no and just sat down?" He dropped a chip.

"No, I'm not kidding. I was hurt."

Shawn loved hearing the stories. He was very close to his brother and it made him feel like Tanner hadn't been gone so long once he knew everything Tanner had been up to. It made him feel part of his life, as if he were there when it all happened.

"Is there anything else that happened after that?" He craved to hear more.

"Oh yes, there's lots more."

"I want to hear it all," he probed.

Rachel looked at her watch, "Oh my, it's 1:00 a.m. and I have to get to bed. If Tanner wakes up and I'm not there he might get worried."

"Yeah, I don't want that," Shawn sounded disappointed, but he didn't want his brother upset either.

"That's okay, I'll tell you some more of the adventures tomorrow, it'll give you something to look forward to."

"That sounds good," he said, pleased.

When Rachel left the room, she was very tired but feeling very hopeful as well. She felt she'd made a friend of Shawn and that's what he needed right now. Once she got to her bed, though, her thoughts began to whirl about whether she is right to keep the secret from Tanner about the razor blade. Even if Shawn was doing well, it would only take one setback and he could be in there cutting himself and they wouldn't know it. It was hard for her to drift off, worried about that thought. Just before she did, she decided that in the morning she would tell Tanner what she saw.

After a good seven hours of sleep, morning came. Rachel woke to the sounds of laughter and dishes clanging downstairs. She was surprised the men weren't already outdoors, working. Hearing the laughter made her even more curious. She figured everyone must be downstairs eating breakfast. Tanner would be waiting for her which meant she'd better hurry. She got dressed and headed down to the kitchen.

"Then, Tanner leaps on the alligator's back, stabbing it in the eye with a knife," Shawn's excited voice echoed through the kitchen. Rachel pushed through the kitchen double doors to see Shawn standing there repeating her stories. Tanner sat at the table with his father, both of them wearing big smiles across their faces as they watched and listened to Shawn's fired up expressions. Victoria stood next to Shawn, watching his every move with a beaming grin across her face.

"Good morning beautiful," Tanner scooted his chair back, ready to stand and give his new bride a morning kiss when she entered the room.

"Go on Shawn, don't let me interrupt," Rachel signaled Tanner to stay seated. She went over to him, giving him a quick little kiss, sitting on his knee, and then giving Shawn her full attention. She was a light thing and she wanted to be close to Tanner during this exciting moment. Tanner loved it and wrapped his arms around her waist.

"First of all, Shawn," Tanner teased, "you probably don't want to be telling mom how I was fighting an alligator." Turning to his parents, Tanner added, "And to tell you the truth, when I was on that alligator's back, I wasn't that brave. I was praying that the alligator didn't reach around and bite my leg off."

Everyone laughed and Shawn went on with his stories. He felt like he was telling everyone things they never knew about Tanner and when it came to his parents, he was. For a good two hours Shawn stood and sat, ate food, poured coffee and laughed, conversing just like a normal 17-year-old. He was making up for lost time. The whole family was overjoyed and feeling like they had the real Shawn back again.

After Shawn finished retelling the stories he had learned from Rachel, Tanner looked at his dad.

"Well, I guess we better get outside and check some more of those grapes," Tanner suggested. Shawn used to like doing that with them. They always teased that if he didn't quit sampling all the grapes while they were working, there wouldn't be any left for making wine.

"You want to come with us, Shawn?" Tanner looked at Shawn as he placed his coffee cup in the sink.

Shawn's face dropped, showing his disappointment. He wanted to go but he knew he couldn't. "No, that's okay," he replied, quickly sounding depressed again. In an instant, Shawn had changed back to that stranger of doom and disappeared back up to his room.

Everyone but Rachel was in shock, staring at the double doors that he had just pushed his way through.

"I blew it didn't I?" Tanner turned to Rachel, very frustrated with himself as if he sent his brother back into depression.

"No, you didn't. It was okay to ask him as long as you accept his answer. He's just not ready for that yet. He's not mad at you, he's mad at himself. It's good. He needs to know what he's missing out on. It will help him strive to get past his phobias so he can eventually do these things. We just don't want to push him if he says no. You did fine." She went over next to him.

"He shut down so quickly and suddenly. Everything was going so well and now he's depressed again," Neil was disappointed, and his voice had changed to that harder tone again.

Cindi Annette

"I tried to explain to all of you that he is going to have ups and downs. Don't let it worry you, he's progressing well. This was a big step, him coming down here, eating and telling stories, and there will be more positives like this. You just have to remember, going out that front door will be the hardest thing he does and also the last thing on his list that he'll want to do. He has lots of hurdles before he'll be ready for that. But he'll get there as long as no one pushes him by trying to force him to soon. Let him go at his own speed. If not, if we nag at him, he'll shut down completely."

Everyone was relieved once Rachel was done explaining what was taking place with Shawn. They all felt better being reminded that there was a plan in place and all of them could help by being positive and patient.

One thing was for sure, Rachel decided not to tell Tanner about the razor blade yet. If he was upset that much just by Shawn going upstairs, depressed, then he really wouldn't handle the razor blade well.

During the day, while the men were working, Rachel went back upstairs to talk to Shawn. She knew he was bothered when he left the kitchen but felt she could help him past it.

She knocked on his door. When he didn't answer right off she asked, "Did you want to hear some more of the adventures involving your brother and everyone?"

Once she said that, Shawn quickly came to the door. It was as if it caused a major change in his moods. "Sure, come in," he signaled.

The room was dark as she entered but he hurried over to the lamp on the desk and turned it on.

Rachel sat down and started telling him about the beach wedding and the emergency that happened during the ceremony. It was a serious one but created a very funny situation.

"My parents were there for that, weren't they?" Shawn asked.

"Yes, they saw it all. Didn't they tell you about it?"

"They tried but I wasn't very receptive at the time. I guess I was mad because Tanner had been away so long," he sounded ashamed.

"That's okay, let's not dwell on the past." She quickly moved on to more stories. She needed him to stay positive in his thoughts.

"At our reception, two guys tried to crash the party. Tanner and I were outside, but Ron, being the Best Man, was ready to throw them out. Of course, they were ready to make a huge fight and ruin the reception but our friend Drake, who is a police officer, stepped in and you should have seen those guys leave quickly," Rachel laughed. Shawn laughed too, ready to hear more.

"After the wedding there was another serious accident involving Rebecca, when all four of us went dune buggy driving," Rachel got his interest but didn't tell the story yet.

"What happened?" he sat, waiting to hear every detail.

Rachel paused, bothered.

"What's wrong?" Shawn asked, confused by her sudden quiet state.

"Shawn," she started to fiddle with her fingers. "I've been bothered about something I saw in your room the first day I came in here and I have to ask you about it."

"What is it?" he asked, bewildered.

"Mind you, I haven't told anyone about this so don't worry. I just want you to tell me the truth about it," she tried hard to get him to be honest with her.

"What?" he was completely baffled.

"I saw a razor blade in your garbage can..." she stated.

"And?" he waited.

"And you aren't...?" She stopped, then looked up from her fidgeting fingers to look in his eyes. She didn't need to say more, the look in her eyes said it all.

"Trying to commit suicide?" he guessed. "No," he said with a chuckle.

"No, not suicide, but you aren't cutting yourself, are you?" She was embarrassed to continue but had to know. This was Tanner's brother and if he was doing that and she hadn't warned Tanner, he'd never forgive her. She'd never forgive herself, either.

"Are you kidding?" he laughed now. He felt complimented that she was worried about him. "I have enough stress with these panic attacks, you think I need pain and sores on top of it?"

"Well, what was the razor blade for?" She knew it wasn't for shaving because it would be in his bathroom, not the garbage can by his desk.

He stood up and walked over to his bedroom windows. They were nice size windows and when the curtains were open, Rachel was sure Shawn could see the whole winery.

He pulled back some of the curtain to reveal a sticker on the window. "I put a sticker on this window when I was little and it seems baked on there after this many years. It drives me crazy, but I can't get it off. Not even with that razor blade." He was frustrated as he pointed to an old sticker that had been scraped over many times.

Rachel could imagine how that would bother him, since looking out that window was his whole life for the past year. She laughed, relieved. "I can help you get that off." She stood up, hurrying over to the window.

"Really? I can't believe a little sticker can be this hard to get off," he squinted his eyes as he looked at the sticker, disturbed.

"It's easy really. All you need is a little Windex and dish soap mixed with some water. Just put a little on a rag, dab it on the sticker, then use a razor blade and it'll come right off. Works great!"

"That's a relief to know."

"You're telling me," Rachel let out with a sigh of relief.

They both laughed and returned to their usual places to get back to more pleasant business.

She went on to tell him about the adventure with the dune buggy crash as he sat listening intently. He would throw in a question now and then. She loved how much he enjoyed the stories and would get involved, making comments like a normal teenager again. It was a good day for her, but not as good for Tanner.

Later that night at dinner, Tanner observed his father being short with his mother again and wondered if they truly were going to be able to fix things between one another.

"I can get my own coffee," Neil snapped, taking his cup back when she picked it up to fill it.

"Fine," she said softly, hoping others wouldn't hear, "you can get your own coffee from now on."

Tanner said nothing, minding his own business but continuing to worry.

***

Several days went by and Shawn was coming down for at least one of his meals every day. His appetite was slowly coming back. He was laughing and talking as Tanner and Rachel kept telling him more stories about their time with Rebecca and Ron. They explained that Shawn would need to know about Rebecca and Ron because they were their closest friends and Rebecca would be visiting soon.

"And Ron might actually come work for us one day," Tanner said, hopeful.

"That'd be great," Shawn replied, pleased, after hearing all the different stories about them both.

"Just remember, he has a bit of a hardcore attitude. He's different than your easy-going brother here," Rachel warned, putting her hand on Tanner's shoulder. "He's a great guy though."

Tanner was feeling pretty good about Shawn's progress and how the day was going, until lunch time came.

Neil had brought a rose for Victoria which put a nice smile on Tanner's face, but not on Victoria's.

"Thank you," she took the rose with a cordial smile, one showing no real feeling. She wanted him to know she was not happy with his up-and-down mood swings. Now Tanner knew what his father meant when he said, "If she'll let me" to Tanner when they discussed his making up with her. He couldn't blame her, though, his father disappearing for three days would make any woman upset and concerned at what her man was doing in those three days. He wondered why his father didn't tell her where he had been? What could he be hiding? He wanted to ask, but he knew his father would sternly say "That's none of your business, son. It's your mother's and mine." He was fortunate to say what he already did to him and get away with it. He wasn't going to push it.

***

Even more time passed and Rachel and Shawn were now playing checkers downstairs by the fireplace at night. The competition grew and eventually Tanner and his dad were playing against the winner. It slowly became a fun family time together. Shawn was no longer just wearing dark clothes. He even let his mother cut his hair one day. Except for refusing to go outside, Shawn was acting like a normal person again.

"I think it's great that Shawn is nearly himself again," Tanner told Rachel as they were getting ready for bed.

"Me too, Tanner, but remember this is just the beginning. He has a long way to go," she warned.

"What do you mean? He's doing great," he looked at her, surprised.

"He doesn't know what's going on in his body or how to handle it. He's distracted at the moment. The first bad panic attack he has will send him right back into that room, scared," she warned as she took off her watch and jewelry and placed them on the nightstand.

"Isn't there a way to teach him how to handle the panic attacks so that doesn't happen?" he asked, confused as to why that hadn't happened yet.

"Yes, there is, but it is a process. Imagine if a person is terrified of needles and has to get a shot, they usually don't want to discuss it at first. It makes them more scared. Panic attacks work the same way. I will discuss with Shawn how to deal with panic attacks but first I thought he needed a break. Kind of like a breath of fresh air. He needs to enjoy life a little again, that way when we talk about dealing with his phobias, it'll be worth it for him to listen even if it's uncomfortable," she explained as she got into bed.

"That makes sense. It shows you how much I don't know about this problem. I'm glad he has you on his side," he admitted, getting into bed next to her and pulling her into his arms. His brother was important to him and the fact that she could relate to all this and help him meant everything to Tanner.

"Don't give me all the credit, you're a big part in this too. You're his big brother and you just being here and setting a good example for him helps tremendously. He loves you a lot and looks up to you. I can tell he yearns to be just like you," she said, looking into his weary brown eyes before kissing him.

"I don't know about all that, but I do know that this big brother shouldn't have been gone nearly as long as I was. Maybe he wouldn't have gotten this bad if I'd have just come home sooner?" he wondered.

"Being gone didn't cause this, Tanner. Being back is going to be a big help in his recovery though. You are supportive and he reaches out to be like you. It keeps him striving to go forward. But there is something deep down that is bothering him and set off his panic attacks to this degree. We know he lost two friends in that car accident, but there's got to be more. People grieve dead friends and loved ones, but he's doing more than that, as if he's hiding something. Maybe he doesn't even realize he's doing it. I don't know, but I do know that somehow I have to draw it out of him if he's ever going to be himself again."

Rachel couldn't help but wonder about what Shawn was hiding. *What is going on in that mind of yours and tearing you apart like this?*

Chapter 6

The next morning arrived quickly and the whole family was finishing up their breakfast when a knock came at the front door.

"I'll get it," Tanner offered, casually getting up to save his parents the effort. Tanner opened the door, and to his surprise, Ron was standing in front of him. A taxi waited in the driveway at the foot of the stairs.

"Ron, I can't believe you're here!" Tanner said, embracing his friend with a manly hug. He and Ron had become the best of friends when they were in Florida.

"Still need a worker?" Ron asked, a little unsure of whether Tanner really needed help or had just offered him the job to be nice, not really expecting Ron to take him up on it.

"Of course we do, you couldn't have timed it more perfectly. The grapes are nearly ready to be harvested and we could use all the help we can get. Come in," Tanner encouraged.

Ron was relieved Tanner actually needed the help and that he appeared thrilled to see him. Travel from Florida would have been a long and expensive trip to come for nothing.

"I need to get my stuff and let the taxi go," Ron informed him.

"Well. let's go get your stuff then," Tanner said agreeably.

They headed down the steps to the taxi and grabbed Ron's luggage. Ron paid for the taxi and they went back inside.

"Rachel, you won't believe who's here," Tanner yelled out from the front door to his new bride. He knew she'd be just as happy to see Ron as he was.

Rachel came quickly through the double doors of the kitchen and the rest of the family followed.

"Ron," she called out, running over and giving him a big hug. She was thrilled to see him. He had a couple of suitcases with him which told her he was staying for a while. *Rebecca will be happy about this*.

"Is this the Ron you've both been telling me about in all the stories?" Shawn asked, in shock, as he came out of the kitchen.

"He's the one," Tanner chuckled, giving Ron a proud pat on the back. "I told him if he ever wanted a job in California, we'd give him one at the winery and here he is."

"That's great, son," Neil came over, happy for Tanner. He knew Ron was the best man at Tanner's wedding and a close friend to his son. He also knew Tanner would enjoy having him in their home.

Victoria was thrilled with all the visitors. She felt like life was starting to feel a little normal again with a house full of people and activity.

Tanner introduced Ron to Shawn and they shook hands with a strong grip.

"I see you're a tough guy like your big brother," Ron teased, smiling at Shawn over the firm handshake. Shawn didn't say anything back, just gave a slight grin. Rachel knew the comment had to have hurt Shawn deep down because he didn't feel like a strong person at the moment. She knew the panic attacks made him feel weak and not like a real man.

"Being a good friend of Tanner, you are welcome to stay here in the main house with family. You don't have to stay in one of the cabins out with the workers. But if you rather stay with the workers that's fine too. Whichever you're most comfortable with is fine with us," Neil offered, as he shook Ron's hand. Tanner could feel his dad's pleasure at having the guest as well.

"Thank you sir, I'll just stay with the workers, that way I don't feel like I'm putting anyone out." Ron replied, but secretly he appreciated the kind offer.

"That's just fine but I insist you come to dinner tonight as our guest. My wife is a great cook." He pulled her next to him, smiling down at her proudly. Victoria gave a half smile. Enough for Ron to believe she was happy with Neil's comment. Tanner was aware of her slight tension; she was still uncomfortable with his unpredictable moods.

"I'll do that, thank you." Ron looked toward Tanner, not knowing where to go or what to do at this point.

"Come on, I'll show you to your cabin. You can get settled in and meet some of the other guys," Tanner signaled towards the door. "You'll like them, they're a great bunch of people."

"Wow, I have to call Rebecca. I wonder if he told her he was coming?" Rachel raised her eyebrows, looking at Shawn while Tanner and Ron went out the door. She couldn't be happier now that both of her friends were going to be nearby.

"Maybe he's trying to surprise her," Shawn warned.

"Good point. I'd better find out first." She took off out the door to catch up with the men.

Shawn's parents looked at Shawn to see his reaction to the new visitor. Shawn headed upstairs, skipping every other step. They hadn't seen him do that in the past year. That was always a happy sign with their boys. When they skipped three steps, something extra special was going on.

"This is going to be great, getting to meet Rebecca and Ron after hearing all these stories about them," Shawn blurted out without looking back as he continued up the stairs. Neil and Victoria looked at one another and smiled.

Rachel found out that Ron had called Rebecca when his plane landed, telling her he was in California. He said she was ecstatic but couldn't arrive until the next day because of her classes and workload. Rachel could relate to that, remembering her big workload. College was nothing like high school. If you get behind, they have no mercy, you're out of the class and then you have to take the whole course over again.

Rachel asked Victoria if there was an extra room where Rebecca could stay while she visited. Victoria was very gracious and more than willing to show Rachel a room for her guest. All the rooms were well kept and decorated beautifully in country decor. Grapes were always involved in any decor at the winery. Rachel couldn't help but feel like she was living in a movie all the time, not actual reality. She and Beth had struggled through many years without parents and having little means to get by; this was way out of her league. In college, life for her was much of the same, just trying to scrimp by all the time. This style of living was something she wasn't accustomed to, but she was acclimating quickly and loving it.

Shawn had stayed in his room since Ron arrived. Rachel began to worry he was feeling like an outcast. She decided she had better check on him.

"Hey Shawn," she knocked on his door.

At first there was silence, then finally a reply. "Yeah?"

"Could you help me move the bed around in the room where Rebecca will be staying?" Rachel wanted to get him out of his room again and involved in doing something. Anything.

"The bed?" He opened the door, looking confused, but he was pleased that she was there and needing his help. He hated feeling useless all the time.

"Yes, I'm sure she'd like the bed closer to the window that way she can look at the stars at night and have the sun shine through first thing in the morning," she explained as they headed for the bedroom Rebecca would be staying in.

She and Shawn spent a good half hour moving things around. Mainly because Rachel wanted Shawn to feel like these were his guests too. She also knew Rebecca would appreciate the changes they made to help her stay to be even more enjoyable.

After dinner, Shawn came down to the large living room and everyone was having a great time. Ron and Tanner were reminiscing about past experiences and Shawn loved hearing Ron's side as well. Tanner's parents sat back, just enjoying all of the conversations.

"Have you and Rebecca been keeping in touch since you've been apart?" Rachel asked Ron as she continued to work on her natural matchmaking skills. It had been about a month that Ron and Rebecca had been apart now and Rachel was interested in an update. She and Rebecca hadn't talked much since Rachel moved back to California. She's been occupied with Shawn, having no time for long phone calls.

Tanner raised an eyebrow at Ron, trying not to laugh. Tanner and Ron were always making jokes about the women and their matchmaking.

"You could say that," Ron said in a hushed tone, as he took a swallow of his beer.

"Oh? What does that mean?" She tried to pry further.

"It means it's none of our business," Tanner quickly interrupted, giving Rachel a furrowed brow.

"What do you think we ought to do when Rebecca gets here?" Ron asked Tanner, changing the subject. "You know she's going to need something fun and wild to do. More wild than fun in her case," he snickered, shaking his head. He was obviously anxious to see her.

"The common thing people do when they visit here is check out the wineries," Victoria suggested.

Tanner, Rachel and Ron all laughed. "I don't think that'll do it for Rebecca. She's going to need something like skydiving or bungee jumping. Anything considerably dangerous," Ron teased. His tone was joking but he was also very serious, knowing Rebecca as he did.

"This is true," Tanner and Rachel echoed with a chuckle.

Victoria looked a little concerned as her motherly instinct showed through.

"Hot air balloon rides would probably be out," Neil teased, recalling their story from the last trip.

"Knowing her, she'd probably be open to it and love it," Tanner agreed.

"But I wouldn't." Rachel quickly shut it down.

"I had a feeling you'd say that." Tanner surrendered the idea quickly.

"How about biking? They have some crazy trails around here. Ones where you can hardly stay on your bike it's so extreme. I've done them and they're really good," Shawn suggested.

"That sounds great! Rough, but not too dangerous where she'll get herself killed." Ron appreciated that thought, looking to Tanner and Rachel for their approval.

"Yeah, it sounds perfect," Rachel agreed and looked at Tanner.

"Let's plan it. Get your laptop and we'll try to find the best place to take her," Tanner suggested.

"I can show you the best ones when you get your laptop. I've been to most of them with my friends," Shawn advised, eager to help.

"Perfect." Tanner was happy to have Shawn involved.

"Better yet, why don't you come with us? You can show us the ropes," Ron suggested, not knowing about Shawn's problem and wanting to include him. He thought he seemed like a nice young man and Ron wouldn't mind getting to know him better.

"No, I can't. Sorry," Shawn's voice went monotone and he stood up from the table.

"You sure man? We could use a good guide," Ron pushed, thinking he might just be shy.

"I'm sure." Shawn's voice dropped as he became embarrassed and quickly left for his room.

Tanner gave Rachel a worried look. It was just like she warned: one minute he was doing good but when going outside is mentioned, he shuts down.

"What'd I say?" Ron could tell he had upset Shawn but he was confused as to why. He felt bad, he was only trying to be nice by including him.

"It's not you. Let's take a walk and we'll fill you in," Tanner said as he stood up from the table, taking Rachel's hand and informing his dad he'd meet up with him outside in a little bit. He didn't want to chance Shawn hearing their discussion.

"Sure." Ron agreed, curious, as he followed Rachel and Tanner outside.

Rachel felt bad. She could see Shawn's curtain move just the slightest bit, enough to know that he was watching them. Rachel pointed at some of the vines in the different fields in the hopes that Shawn would not catch on to their topic.

After Tanner was done explaining to Ron about Shawn's problems, it didn't go as well as Rachel had hoped. Ron's immediate opinion was that everyone was coddling Shawn and that's why he was having these problems. If they'd just force him to confront his phobias, he would get past them, he figured. Rachel tried to explain that he needed to face his phobias but at his own speed and not by people pushing him. Ron completely disagreed. He believed in tough love, the way he was brought up. He claimed that it made him the strong man he is today and that the same would work for Shawn.

Tanner made it clear to Ron that Rachel had been the only one who has even been able to get Shawn out of his shell in a year. He didn't want Ron interfering and he certainly didn't want Ron being rough on him in any manner.

"Just let her handle Shawn," Tanner told him, making a suggestion at this point rather than a demand. If Ron didn't get the hint, then Tanner would lay down the law.

"All right, it's your place and your brother, I'll stay out of it." Ron backed down, realizing he was out of line. He didn't mean to bring division between them when he had just arrived. He just really felt their way wasn't going to help Shawn. But it was none of his business and he knew that.

Rachel was glad for Tanner's support but also very worried that Ron might cause some future problems when it came to Shawn. He felt his tough love would work and she knew it was the worst thing in Shawn's case. She could only hope that he really would respect Tanner's wishes and not interfere.

***

The next morning, Tanner loaned Ron his Mustang to pick up Rebecca from the train station. She lived and worked by a college, having no use for a car nor the expense of one. The minute they arrived at the winery, Tanner and Rachel hurried out to the Mustang to greet her.

"Rebecca, I'm so happy you're here," Rachel said, thrilled, as she gave her friend a big hug. Rebecca was a beautiful redhead, about 5'6" tall with a great body, and she was dressed like a college student. She wore her hair in a ponytail with a cap and was wearing blue jeans and a tight t-shirt with some number on it that pertained to her university sports team. Rebecca was happy to be with her friends again and ready to give Tanner a hard time.

"Someone was supposed to bring Rachel to come visit me right when they got back from their honeymoon and didn't," she complained. She wasn't really mad but had to give Tanner a hard time.

"Sorry, about that Rebecca. We just bought a new car and I was about to bring her when Ron appeared and changed our plans." Tanner gave her a welcoming hug, knowing her growl was worse than her bite.

"Well, I'll forgive you this time since we're all together again," she said with a smile. She was totally content just to have all four of them in one place. They had such fun in Florida before Tanner and Rachel left for their honeymoon, she was anxious to get that fun started again. Minus the part when she got knocked out in a dune buggy crash.

"Let's go inside. You can say hi to my family and get settled in your room," Tanner suggested.

"Sounds good." She wrapped her arm around Rachel's arm, thrilled to be back together once more, and headed inside. Ron looked at Tanner and threw up his arms as if to say, 'That's my girlfriend, leaving me behind to be a bellboy.' Tanner laughed. *That's how those two always act together, bantering back and forth. Things hadn't changed in a month.*

Rachel could see Shawn's curtain move the tiniest bit in the upstairs window again. "You're going to like Shawn," she mentioned to Rebecca. "He's very excited to meet you. He feels he knows you and Ron already because of all the stories we've told him."

"That's a scary thought," Rebecca snickered, teasing Rachel. "But then again, I guess a teenager would love those kinds of stories."

"Remember though, as I explained on the phone, he struggles with anxiety so don't take it personally if he won't speak to you or suddenly walks out when you're talking to him."

Rachel wanted Rebecca prepared when she first met Shawn. She felt confident Rebecca could be a big help when it came to Shawn. She had always been supportive of Rachel through the years with her panic attacks.

When they entered the front door, Neil and Victoria were ready and waiting to greet their newest guest. Neil had his arm around Victoria like a loving husband, but Tanner could tell his mother was only tolerating it. She was still upset with him.

"Nice to see you again, Rebecca," Neil shook her hand politely with a welcoming smile. He quickly announced that he had work to do and left out the front door. Victoria rolled her eyes, but tried to hide it.

"We're pleased you could come. Make yourself at home," Victoria greeted her with a gentle hug.

Rachel could see Shawn at the top of the stairs but he wasn't showing any sign of coming down.

"Hey Shawn, this is Rebecca, she's anxious to meet you," Rachel called up to him, hoping he'd come down.

Everyone was quiet, staring up at him as he stood at the top of the stairs. It was just for a moment, until Rebecca made her move.

"Hi Shawn, you don't have to come all the way down here, I can come up. I need exercise after that long train ride." She rapidly went up the stairs, skipping two steps at a time and stopping right in front of him with her hand out. "Hi, I'm Rebecca."

"Hi, I'm Shawn, nice to meet you." He shook her hand and a smile crossed his face. He was surprised that she came up the stairs as she did just to meet him, but he liked it.

"Rachel tells me you two are good friends. She also said you're hard to beat at checkers." Rebecca tried for a conversation.

Shawn kept his smile but didn't comment back. He was concerned that a conversation might turn into embarrassment like it did with Ron.

"How about this stair rail?" she whispered to him. "How many times have you gone down this?" She looked anxious to try it out.

"A lot," he replied with a chuckle. He and Tanner had spent many days racing down that rail as kids.

"Oh really?" She looked at both rails then back at him. "We'll just have to test it out one night when everyone's asleep and see who's faster," she challenged him in a whispered voice, keeping her plan secret.

He grinned, accepting the challenge and seeing for himself that she was the wild and fun person Rachel described her to be.

"Okay Rebecca, are you already up there scheming with Shawn? I see you whispering!" Rachel called up, teasing her. Tanner glanced Rachel's way, impressed by Rebecca. She was already getting somewhere with Shawn.

Ron, on the other hand, looked irritated. He didn't have a clue how to relate to a person with this kind of problem. He was brought up in a very rough environment and all he knew was that you had to be tough to make it in life. He didn't like they were babying Shawn (as he felt they were doing) and he didn't like that his girlfriend was joining in with it. He was trying to stay out of it like Tanner asked but already he could tell it was going to be hard to ignore.

"Rebecca's room is the last room on the left from the top of the stairs," Tanner directed Ron so he could bring her suitcase up for her. "When you're done helping her get settled, I'll take you around the winery while the women catch up on their girl talk."

Rebecca watched as Ron came up the stairs. It had been over a month since they saw each other so she was longing to spend time with him. However, she did want some girl time with Rachel too. She had been talking with Ron nearly every night on the phone that whole past month. They had exchanged many emails and Ron even sent her some gifts. She still couldn't wait to feel his arms around her, like at the airport when he picked her up. They had embraced, passionately kissed, and held each other close. It felt good and she wanted more.

Chapter 7

Once Rebecca and Ron got into her bedroom, Ron couldn't hold it in any longer.

"I wish you wouldn't join in with Tanner and Rachel, babying Shawn like this. I don't see how everyone doesn't see that it's just making him worse," he placed the suitcase on the ground by the closet, not knowing for sure where Rebecca would want it.

Rebecca was shocked by Ron's bitterness on the subject. *How does he have such a strong opinion when he just got here?*

"How do you know that, Ron?" she questioned casually, as she looked around the lovely room in awe. It had a large bed with a fluffy bedspread, four pillows, a loveseat, a desk, a huge walk in closet, and its own fireplace. She was used to an apartment with close quarters and was happy when it had a bathroom bigger than a closet. This was the opposite. To her, it was a castle. She walked over to look out the window which showed a beautiful view of the winery. *I'm going to love it here and never want to go home.* It was hard for her to focus on what Ron was worried about at the moment when she was surrounded by sheer pleasures.

"It doesn't take long to know what's going on," he continued. "He didn't even come down the steps to greet you. Come on, how hard can that be to figure out? He should have been told to get his butt down there and properly introduce himself. If he didn't, Tanner should have made him."

"I didn't care, I went up to him." She spoke like it was an easy solution which only made him more irritated.

"The kid won't even walk outside," his voice got loud as his frustration built.

"Shhhh," she put her finger over her mouth as she tiptoed over to him. Shawn's room was close by, she didn't want him to hear them talking.

He lowered his voice and continued, "If they'd just throw him outside and make him get busy working he'd forget all about his problems."

"I'm sure they've probably already tried distracting him with work and it must not have helped," she countered.

"Then they're not making him work hard enough."

"He's having attacks. Those are not just something that distractions can prevent. He needs to learn how to handle the attacks."

"Nonsense. I've had panic attacks myself and no one taught me how to deal with them. I just got past them eventually."

Rebecca knew she was getting nowhere with Ron at the moment. He was being unreasonable. Maybe if she could get him involved with her and other things for a little bit he would calm down and then he'd actually listen to what she had to say.

"Ron, we haven't seen each other in a long time, is this really what you want to be talking about right now?" She moved in close to him and began rubbing his shoulders and down his arms.

His face quickly softened; he didn't even need to think about it. Realizing that this wasn't what was important to him at that moment, he quickly wrapped his arms around her, holding her tight as a smile crossed his face. "No, it is not," he said, giving her a welcoming kiss.

"I didn't think so," she said in a seductive tone as she returned his kiss. She had missed Ron, it felt like forever since they had seen each other. Holding each other at the airport wasn't quite enough.

"I'm glad you're here," Ron whispered, as he took his finger and gently moved a strand of hair away from her eyes as he peered into them.

"I'm glad you're here," she whispered back as she slowly rubbed her hand up the center of his chest, stopping when she felt his heart beating fast against it.

He took her hand from his chest, kissing it ever so gently, then he kissed her lips once more, passionately this time. Her lips were warm and inviting and he never wanted to let go of her. She returned the passion as she leaned her body into his. When their breathing began to intensify, she suggested, "We had better get out of here before we get carried away."

"That'd be okay with me," he gave her a seductive smile and another kiss.

"I bet it would," she teased, having a hard enough time convincing herself to pull away. "Come on Romeo, calm down," she teased, as she finally gave him a gentle push and backed away. "I really need to visit with Rachel for a bit. I want to hear about her honeymoon trip and we are their guests here, it's only polite for me to visit with her when I arrive," she explained, trying to be careful of his feelings. "Can you help Tanner for a little while and then we'll meet up later?"

"Sure," he surrendered. He figured he wasn't going anywhere, this is where he'd be living now for a while, he could wait.

The men went out into the winery while the two women went into Rachel's room and talked for two hours straight. Rachel told Rebecca about the fun and exciting adventures that she and Tanner had on their honeymoon. Rebecca laughed, loving all the details. It made her feel as if she were right there watching everything as it happened.

"I got you a special gift, like I promised." Rachel walked over to her dresser, opened the second drawer, and pulled out two gift-wrapped packages. "Actually, two gifts." She brought them over to Rebecca who was sitting comfortably on Rachel's bed with a big smile on her face. She handed her the smaller gift first. Rebecca loved surprises.

"What is it?" She quickly opened the small package before Rachel could even begin to answer.

The first gift was a Black Hills gold bracelet with charms that Rachel had carefully selected just for Rebecca. One charm represented the Milky Way galaxy. Others were diamond-shaped stars and pearl moons.

"Oh, this is beautiful Rachel, I love it!" She jumped up, giving Rachel a big hug as she insisted Rachel help her to get the bracelet on her wrist.

"I got this gift in Kauai too. I thought it'd be fun for you to wear when you're at college." Rachel handed her the bigger package.

It was a t-shirt that read: 'Don't rush me, I'm waiting for the last minute.'

Rebecca busted up laughing. "This is great. I can tease my instructors by wearing this shirt."

She had been going to that college for years now and those instructors all knew her well. Rachel figured they would probably get a kick out of her shirt.

Rachel updated Rebecca on what had been going on with Shawn and let her know that anything she wanted to do to help with the situation was welcome. That might be a dangerous thing to say to Rebecca, but Rachel knew that she was good with these types of problems.

Time was running out and the men were due back in the house soon and Rachel hadn't heard any juicy details on Ron and Rebecca's relationship yet.

"Now, before the men get here, fill me in on what's been going on between you and Ron!" Rachel sat up taller on the bed, giving Rebecca her full attention.

A smile crossed Rebecca's face.

"Tell me," Rachel urged. "Start with what happened when we left for our honeymoon and you two were left without us for those few days."

"At first I was disappointed because he told me right off he wasn't going to let me do anything physical. No rollerblading, he said, or bungee jumping. Not even bumper cars at an amusement park. He claimed that he promised you both and he wasn't going to be any part of me getting hurt again." She gave Rachel a playful angry look.

"If I know Ron, I'm sure he thought of somewhere to take you to have a good time. He's not the type of guy to let a woman down, especially one like you." Rachel told her confidently. "He must have thought of something fun for you both to do?" she challenged, defending Ron.

"He did," she said with a sly look. "He took me to a romantic river boat dinner show with dancing and live music. He actually got dressed up again like the wedding. Not in a full suit or anything, but he rented a sports jacket and tie. He was very handsome, and it was very romantic. I didn't expect him to be romantic like that, to be honest. He has many layers to his personality, I'm learning."

"I am beginning to see that too. Go on," Rachel said, arching her brows.

"One of the days, he took me to some beautiful gardens. We followed all these paths seeing different kinds of plants and birds. It was vibrant in colors and very relaxing just strolling around. The place was huge, you could get lost in it. We actually did a couple of times," Rebecca giggled. "But we didn't care. He held his arm around me as we just talked and got to know each other better. Did you know he was a fireman for a while?"

"You're kidding? No, I didn't know that."

"He had to quit. Something to do with his dad needing his help. It took him a long time to become one and once he did, he had to quit which I could tell was disappointing to him." Rebecca was a little suspicious of that event. She felt Ron wasn't telling her everything when it came to his dad.

"That's too bad."

"Anyway, we talked about all kinds of things he's done as an adult. He's done lots of different labor jobs. He even worked on a fishing boat for a period of time. But somehow, he kept coming back to help his dad. I'm thinking maybe his dad has a health problem or something.

He didn't tell me much about his childhood, but little comments that slipped out told me it wasn't good. He seems to avoid it like the plague. I figure he'll tell me in his own time."

"I don't know much about him either, except that the guy seems to have a big heart, wanting to help others. He must have had a rough upbringing, judging by the tough guy attitude he carries around with him. I know his dad is bad news, from what Aunt Flora and Harvey told me when I was staying in Florida."

"What did they say?" Rebecca wanted any information she could get.

"Basically, they told me to stay clear of the dad, that he was trouble. They also said he treats Ron horribly. I don't know much else, but I do know that scar above his eye came from his dad."

"What? Really? I'll have to pursue it when the time is right," she put her hand on her chin, thinking.

"What else did you guys do?" Rachel wanted to get back on a positive topic.

"He rented a motel room the night after spending the day at the gardens," Rebecca continued.

"He what?" Rachel was concerned Ron made that advance pretty early into their relationship.

"Not for us to stay in," Rebecca laughed, "just so we could go on their beach at night. Ron made a fire and actually cooked me a steak dinner with corn on the cob and wine. He brought a radio and played romantic music. We watched the waves in the moonlight and had such a great time just being together. We were there until 2:00 a.m. talking and just relaxing. He told me so many crazy, funny things he's done and I told him some of the crazy things you and I have done."

"You were the crazy one. I was always the one with a level head trying to keep us out of trouble," Rachel corrected her playfully.

"This is true. Anyway, back to my story. The last day we spent by the piers. You know how I love shopping. They had vendors everywhere and anything I looked twice at, Ron wanted to buy for me. There were street performers everywhere and live music, and all kinds of different foods, we stuffed ourselves tasting everything. It was an incredible day. By the time he took me to the airport, I was exhausted and I slept most of the way home. Since then, we pretty much have talked and emailed each other every day. He even sent me roses and bought me a new iPhone."

"What? He bought you an iPhone?"

"Yes, I dropped mine in the toilet one day and it was a goner."

"You dropped it in the toilet? How did..."

"Don't ask. When he didn't hear from me for a couple of days until I bought a burner phone he said he couldn't have that and shipped me a new iPhone with two day air. This one," Rebecca held it up. It was without a doubt an expensive phone. Something she could never afford on her own with her pay.

"Wow," Rachel was impressed.

"When I first got back to California, we talked all night three nights in a row. I had trouble staying awake in my classes to say the least. We had to quit doing that."

"It's amazing that you don't know his whole life story in that amount of time," Rachel commented.

"A lot of times we just talked about our day and our hobbies, music… things like that. He didn't like to talk about his younger years as a child. What little he revealed was just to say he worked at the hardware store growing up and lost his mom when he was young. He avoided any deep discussions and I never wanted to push him on the subject. Ron doesn't seem like the kind of guy you want to push too far."

"I think he's just as fearful of pushing you too far sometimes," Rachel said with a chuckle. "You two make a perfect pair."

"He's got a soft side too, though. Sometimes when I wrote him an email and I was feeling down, he would email me back saying sweet things making me feel better. He'd even send a silly video to make me laugh."

"Really!" Rachel got a kick out of hearing more about Ron's soft side. She knew he had one because he'd helped her in the past. She recalled the snake incident. He thought Rachel was hilarious, running around scared of a snake, but he took care of her still. He made sure the snake was caught and checked the whole pet store for any more. Hearing Rebecca's stories revealed yet another interesting side of this mysterious friend of theirs.

Eventually, Tanner and Ron came back in from roaming the winery. Tanner went upstairs to encourage the women to come down for lunch. As they headed down the hall, Rachel stopped at Shawn's door and knocked.

"Lunch is on, Shawn." She was hoping to encourage him to join them, not wanting Ron's earlier comment to make him avoid everyone.

Rebecca joined in, trying to encourage him to come down. "I was hoping to challenge you to a game of checkers downstairs after lunch. I want to see just how good you are."

To their surprise, it worked. He opened the door and joined the group. Rachel was very relieved. She didn't want any more setbacks this early on with Ron and Rebecca's visit.

During lunch, Tanner's parents spent most of the time questioning Rebecca and Ron to learn more about them. That kept Shawn out of the spotlight which helped him stay relaxed.

While everyone was listening to Ron and Rebecca, Neil reached for Victoria's hand on the table next to his in hopes that she wouldn't pull away. It was a gesture of love he was trying to show. To Tanner's surprise she let him hold her hand and even gave him a slight smile when he did.

After lunch, Rebecca gave Ron a quick kiss and headed out of the kitchen to go play checkers with Shawn. Ron, however, followed close behind. Rebecca figured Ron must have had other ideas for her, based on the disappointed look on his face. She could understand his feelings, after all, he hadn't seen her since Florida and she already put him off once today.

"I'm just going to play checkers for a little bit while Tanner shows you around the winery some more." She figured with Ron just starting work at the winery there must be a lot for Tanner to show him. "When you come back, you can take me on a private tour, just you and me." She gave him an enticing look, hoping that the suggestion would make Ron happy again. It worked. A grin crossed his face at the thought of the private tour.

Tanner put his dishes in the sink and gave his mom a kiss on the check, thanking her for the nice lunch. He then strolled over to Rachel, giving her a warm kiss. "I have to get back to work. I'll see you later." He gave her a flirtatious smile.

"I'll be waiting," she said in an alluring whisper. Romance was not lacking between these two newlyweds.

Rachel, Rebecca, and Shawn took turns competing at checkers and playing the winner of each game. They were laughing and having a great time. Shawn was winning nearly every game. He was really good with his strategy. It was impressive to Rebecca and made for a good challenge. After a couple of hours, Rachel suggested that she and Rebecca had better go find their men before they start missing them. She didn't want Ron to have any more cause for complaint against Shawn. Rebecca was the type to get wrapped up in a game and not think about anything else. It was up to Rachel to keep her alert to other things around her like Ron and keeping him happy.

When Rachel and Rebecca found Tanner, he was sitting in the driver's seat on what Rachel would have called a big tractor. "It's called a mechanical harvester," Tanner told her. He was pushing buttons on what looked like a monitor.

"This machine will vibrate the grapes off the vines during the harvest, saving us a lot of time and money," Tanner continued. The two women were properly impressed with the machine.

"Remember when I explained to you before that this machine can't fit down all the rows of vines? Some rows are close together or on steep hills which means they have to be picked by hand."

"Yes, I remember," Rachel replied.

"That's why my dad and Ron are over there working on the smaller tractors," he pointed at them on the other side of the building. "Those tractors are going to pull gondolas for the pickers to fill with grapes. They have to make sure those tractors are in perfect running order before the harvest. It can set us way back if one of them breaks down in the middle of the harvesting."

Tanner enjoyed explaining to Rachel how things worked when it came to the winery. He had missed working there for the past six years, except for harvest time when he'd fly home to help out. He knew his family counted on him at that time of year plus he never wanted to miss out on the tradition. He carried fond memories from those days growing up.

"Will you be driving this during the harvest?" Rachel asked, wondering to herself what she would be doing while he was up on that machine.

He jumped down from the machine, landing next to her. "Nope, Sanchez will be doing that while I'll oversee all of the picking by hand. You, Ron, and I will all be together with the workers, picking grapes. We'll be filling crates and the big gondolas. At different times I'll be driving one of those tractors," he gestured to where Neil and Ron were working. "You can ride up here with me. It's all a lot of work but a lot of fun too."

Rachel felt good knowing that Tanner was eager to work together with her as husband and wife. He pulled her close to him and they looked out over the grapevines together, thinking ahead to that day.

Rebecca had hurried over to Ron and Neil to watch them work. She wanted to tease Ron about the overalls he had changed into since she last saw him. It was clear they were to protect him from the black grease he already had smeared on them, but she still enjoyed any excuse to give him a hard time.

"Hey, Mr. Green Jean?" she teased when she got close to him.

"Who is Mr. Green Jean?" he questioned, not understanding her joke but knowing it was some sort of ribbing about the way he was dressed.

"Didn't you ever watch TV as a kid?" she teased.

"Apparently not the same TV shows you watched," he shot back.

Rebecca was walking back over to Tanner and Rachel when an idea popped into her head about the harvest day. "I want to help with the harvest! It sounds like a lot of fun." She wanted to be included in their plan. She didn't want to miss out on such a big event.

"What about your classes?" Rachel asked, knowing that this would cause problems for her.

"I'll email my instructors. I can arrange to do most of the work online and anything I miss I'll arrange to work double-time to make up. They know I'm dependable with my assignments; they'll work with me."

Rachel knew that to be true. She and Rebecca always took their classes seriously.

"That's going to be a lot of homework for you," Rachel warned, knowing the pressure herself from trying to keep up while she was in Florida. Rachel wanted her to stay, it would be fun for all of them, she just didn't want her friend to get herself into a stressful situation.

"Don't worry, I'll be fine. I do need to ask you for something else though," Rebecca changed the subject. "I need some things from the store if I'm staying longer, can you give me a lift before dinner?"

"You're welcome to use our car to drive there. The stores are all right down the main road from here. All you have to do is follow the street out front and you'll drive right to them. Will you be okay alone? I'd like to stay and help Victoria get dinner ready for everyone, if that's good with you? It's just her alone doing everything," Rachel explained. Tanner pulled his car keys from his pocket and tossed them to Rebecca.

"I'll be fine." She caught the keys then added, "You're trusting me to drive your new car?" She teased Tanner with a lifted brow. Rachel gave her a warning look.

"I'll be back in a flash. I just need a few things," she said with a smirk, then thanked Tanner for the keys. "Are you sure you don't need my help fixing dinner Rachel? I can shop after dinner if you need me to."

"No, two of us can get it done, that's fine. You go get what you need."

As Rebecca started to walk away, a couple of workers drove past, each driving a quad. Rebecca's eyes lit up as she turned looking at Tanner with an eager look on her face.

"No," he said sternly, shaking his head at her. "Not happening! Don't think about it."

Rachel laughed as Rebecca frowned and walked away.

A couple of hours later, dinner was ready and Rebecca still wasn't back. Rachel wasn't surprised, Rebecca loves to shop and these were new stores for her.

Tanner and Ron came in from working, ready to eat a big dinner. Victoria was still hovering over the food platters that she and Rachel had prepared. She wanted everything to be just right for her new guests. They had prepared a big lasagna, salad, garlic bread, and a fruit cobbler for dessert. One thing was sure, in Victoria's household the men were fed well for all their hard work.

"Where is your father?" Victoria asked Tanner as he and Ron sat down at the table. Victoria didn't like her men to be late for their meals. She wanted them to eat while the food was hot and tasty.

"He said to tell you he'd be right in, he had something he wanted to check on with one of the tractors before he stopped for the day," Tanner answered.

Victoria glanced out the window, looking to see if she could see him coming. It wasn't like him to be late. He was a man that believed in being punctual.

Shawn entered the room. Tanner and Ron greeted him as he took a seat at the table.

"How's it going, Buddy?" Tanner gave Shawn a little slug to the arm.

"Fine," Shawn replied, keeping his conversation short. Rachel could tell he felt guilty about not being outside and helping with all the hard work.

As Shawn stood up to head for the coffee pot, a hard, loud knock came at the front door followed by the doorbell ringing over and over again without a break. It startled everyone, something had to be wrong for someone to be that persistent and loud.

Tanner hurried to the front door and Ron and Shawn followed right behind him.

"Mr. Reed is in big trouble, come quick!" Juan's voice trembled as he took off his hat, showing respect for his boss. His hands shook and his face was pale. Tanner knew it had to be something dreadful. He glanced back sharply as terror lit up his own face.

"Take me to him," he told Juan, not wanting to waste any time. Ron and Shawn followed without hesitation. Juan rushed over to the barn where the tractors were kept. Rachel and Victoria followed as quickly as they could, trying to keep up. They didn't hear all of what was going on but they knew something was wrong and it concerned Neil. They knew it had to be serious, the way the men were acting and when it came to machinery, Victoria knew the dangers that could be involved. They've only had a few incidents throughout the years but when they did, they were usually serious ones.

"Boss... working tractor. Arm stuck... in engine, bleeding bad." Juan tried to communicate through his broken English as they rushed to reach Neil.

"That sounds bad," Tanner muttered. "Mom, call 911 right away," he yelled as he picked up his pace.

With shaking hands, Victoria pulled her cell phone out of her pocket and dialed 911.

Chapter 8

Neil was in the big barn where all of the tractors were stored for maintenance. As they marched in, Rachel noticed that some of the tractors around them were taken apart. Upon reaching Neil, Rachel could see that his arm was stuck in a large tractor engine of some sort. She had no clue what kind of machine it was, there were so many in the building and they were all foreign to her. Neil looked very pale and was losing blood rapidly. She felt faint just seeing him in that state.

"Dad!" Shawn ran over to his father, panicked.

"It's okay son, I just got myself a little stuck here," Neil tried not to scare his son. Neil was shocked to see Shawn outside and knew how hard it had to be for him, but then to also see him in this state had to be overwhelming.

Tanner quickly assessed the situation and it was bad.

"Get a socket set," Tanner told Antonio, another worker who had arrived to help. "Ron, give me your belt," he ordered, needing to make a tourniquet to stop the bleeding. Ron immediately removed his belt, and handed it to Tanner. "Shawn, get me a crow bar." He gave orders quickly, knowing there was no time to spare. "Get me a big wrench," he told a second worker that had arrived.

"Hold on Dad, I'll get you out of there, don't worry," he promised. Tanner's hands shook as he worked rapidly to get the belt around Neil's upper arm to make the tourniquet. Shaking or not, it didn't slow him down. He knew his dad could die if he lost too much blood.

"I know you will, son. Don't worry, my arm is numb right now. I don't feel any pain," Neil said, regretting that his sons had to deal with this horrible situation. His voice was weak and being numb didn't sound like a good sign to Tanner.

Shawn and the other workers returned promptly with their items.

"I've got this," Ron told Tanner as he reached over, grabbing the wrench and socket set. He could see from the tools that Tanner had asked for that he was planning to take the engine apart in order to get his dad's arm out. It would be the safest way to prevent more damage and bleeding.

"Put the crow bar right in this spot here," Tanner directed Shawn. "We want to make sure the engine doesn't crunch down on his arm any more."

"You got it," Shawn replied, doing just as he was told.

Victoria came into the building after calling 911 and instantly panicked. "Neil!" she screamed. Tears shot down her face as she ran towards him. Her emotions were out of control and her face quickly went pale.

"Rachel, take her outside. Don't let her in here," Tanner snapped as he grabbed his mother and turned her towards the exit. He gave Rachel a sharp look that meant *don't let my mom see this*.

"Watch for the ambulance," Tanner encouraged.

"Come on, Victoria," Rachel gently grabbed her, knowing that Tanner was right. No woman needed to see her man go through this misery.

"No!" Victoria fought Rachel, turning back towards her husband once more.

"Victoria, I'm okay. Our boys will get me out, don't worry. Go with Rachel," his voice was weak and it took everything he had to comfort his wife before he passed out. Rachel had Victoria were already headed towards the exit and Tanner was glad that she didn't see Neil faint.

Shawn was startled when his dad passed out, not knowing if he was still alive.

"He's okay Shawn, he just passed out. It's expected in an accident like this," Tanner tried to convince Shawn as well as himself as he continued to work to free his dad. They needed to focus on that right now, not losing their heads.

"He's all right," Ron agreed, trying to assure them both that Neil was okay at the moment. The tourniquet had stopped the bleeding and he knew it was common for a person to become unconscious in this kind of trauma.

"Victoria, we have to let them get him out," Rachel continued to talk in an effort to distract her. "We need to help by watching for the rescue trucks or they won't know which building he's in."

"Have her get some clean rags while you wait for the ambulance." Ron yelled out.

"Okay," Victoria yelled back, picking up on the request and readily hurrying to the house to get the rags. She figured rags would be a necessity with an injury such as this, she needed to hurry.

Tanner and Ron worked together, one on each side of the engine, taking it apart as fast as their hands could move. Neil came to again and it was Shawn's job to keep his mind occupied while Tanner and Ron worked.

Rachel was glad for Victoria to have something to do as she watched anxiously for the fire department which she was sure would arrive first.

Victoria was back in a flash with rags. She handed them off to a worker to bring to Tanner inside. Victoria was crying and shaking as Rachel put her arms around her, promising her that Tanner would get Neil out and begging her not to worry. Deep down, Rachel desperately wanted the rescue vehicles to get there to help Tanner. She knew this had to be a horrible thing for him to deal with, watching his own dad stuck in this engine and bleeding badly.

Something happened and Neil let out with a loud yell of pain. Rachel and Victoria looked at each other in shock.

Victoria tried to push past Rachel to get inside, worried for her husband. Rachel stood her ground. It was the only thing she could do to help Tanner.

"No, Victoria, you don't want to go in there. Let the men get him out." Rachel also knew that whatever was going on in there, neither one of them would want to see.

"I'm his wife, I should be by his side," she pleaded, feeling guilty and helpless.

"I know how you must feel. I wanted to be in the pond when Tanner was in there with alligators, but it would have made things worse for him if I was. He would have been worried about me instead of taking care of himself. It will make things worse for Neil if you go in there right now. He's not alone, he has his sons with him," Rachel tried to reason with her. Victoria again surrendered to her wishes, knowing what Rachel said was true and that she didn't want to make things worse for her husband.

Sirens were heard in the distance as Shawn came running out of the building with blood splattered on his shirt. "Tanner and Ron got his arm out," he announced, out of breath but pleased at their progress.

"Is he okay? I heard him scream!" Victoria asked, grabbing his arm.

"That happened when they got him out, but Tanner said it was a good sign because his arm had been numb until then," Shawn tried to calm her concerns.

His mother quickly ran inside the building now, there was no stopping her. She had waited long enough and it was time to be by her man's side.

"He needs the ambulance," Shawn told Rachel. "He lost a lot of blood." As he spoke, two fire trucks and an ambulance drove onto the property. Shawn ran down the driveway, waving his arms in the air to get their attention as to which direction to come. There were different buildings and roads and Shawn didn't need the firetrucks lost. Time was of the essence. The firetrucks and ambulance followed Shawn's directions.

Upon arriving at the proper building, they pulled up urgently and the EMTs along with the firefighters leaped out of their vehicles, grabbing their gear and rushing with Shawn into the building.

It wasn't long and they were wheeling Neil out on a stretcher. His arm was bandaged with heavy layers. Victoria held Neil's good hand as she walked next to the stretcher. Shawn, Ron, and Tanner trailed behind as Tanner spoke to one of the EMTs. Between Tanner's exhausted appearance and the blood splashed on his shirt, Rachel knew it had to have been a tedious process to free Neil's arm. Tanner could be proud of himself and all the men because she could hear as the EMT spoke to Tanner.

"All of you did a great job. Putting the tourniquet on was a must and if you tried getting it his arm out without taking the engine apart, things could have gotten a lot worse, very fast," the EMT told him.

"I'm glad to hear that, but I certainly hope I never have to do something like that again."

The EMT gave him an amused grin.

"I love you, Dad," Shawn said, worried for his father, but relieved that he now has medical attention.

"I'm proud of you, son," Neil moaned to Shawn. He was pale and weak but he wanted his son to know how much it meant to him that Shawn had pushed his phobias aside to be there for him.

The EMTs loaded Neil into the ambulance and Tanner assured his father that the family would meet him at the hospital.

Everyone raced toward the house to clean up and head for the hospital. Ron hurried to his cabin to change before Rebecca returned.

Tanner told his mother, "The EMT said that he has seen a lot worse and that dad should be okay." He tried to comfort her as she grabbed her keys and purse, ready to head for the hospital. Her hands were still shaking and tears filled her eyes. "I don't think you should drive alone. Why don't you take Shawn with you," Tanner suggested.

"I'm not going," Shawn said with a flat tone and took off up the stairs.

"What?" Tanner was totally confused. One minute Shawn was outside and normal and the next, this again. Rachel quickly hurried over to Tanner, knowing how stressed he was.

"I'm fine, I don't want anyone to go with me," Victoria said and out the door she went. Her mind was set on getting to her husband and not wasting any time.

"I don't get it. You won't believe all the stuff Shawn did helping me and Ron to get my dad out, and now he's too scared to go to the hospital?" Tanner was very confused.

"Ups and downs, remember?" she reminded him. "When there's an emergency, a person with phobias is focused on someone else. The minute the emergency is over they're focused back on their own feelings. He was there when you needed him. Let's not turn it to a negative. Go change and let's get to the hospital. I'll call Rebecca and ask her to keep an eye on Shawn,"

"Okay, I guess." Tanner tried to calm himself and be understanding but it was hard because he was very emotional over the whole situation with his dad and Shawn. He hurried upstairs to change and wash up as quickly as he could. He knew his parents needed him at the hospital. Rachel wanted to stay with Shawn, she knew his head and heart had to be pulling him in every direction at the moment, but she needed to be there for her husband too. She was going to have to rely on Rebecca to help her with Shawn. Rachel called Rebecca as she waited in the car for Tanner. She explained everything that had happened since Rebecca had left for the store.

"I hate leaving him right now but Tanner needs me at the hospital. It was horrible what Shawn saw and went through with his dad. I'm afraid it might be enough to set him back when he's been making such good progress. I'm really worried," she told Rebecca.

"Don't worry, I'll talk to him," Rebecca assured her. "Call me the minute you have an update on Neil."

"I will, thank you, I'm so glad you're here," Rachel told her, then hung up.

On the way to the hospital, Tanner brought up the discussion about Shawn again.

"You've been a real help with Shawn, Rachel. We all really appreciate it. As you can tell, we don't have a clue how to help with this type of situation. It's hard to understand his moods and thoughts, I never know what to do or not do. It's so easy for me to get frustrated with him and I don't want to do that and make him relapse."

"You're all doing just fine. The most important thing you can do is keep being patient and supportive. Realize that he's going to have ups and downs right now. If there were no ups, we'd have something to worry about," she explained, "but he's giving us lots of ups."

"That's true. We've seen a lot of improvement since you've been working with him," Tanner agreed, as he turned the car into the hospital parking lot. Even though it was a confusing process, he knew he had to support it because it was working and that's what mattered.

***

Rebecca arrived back at the winery twenty minutes after Rachel phoned her. Ron had changed his shirt and cleaned up before she arrived. He hurried over to her car when she drove up. She got out, throwing her arms around him and holding him tight. "I'm so sorry to hear you went through all that and I wasn't here for you."

"That's okay. It was probably better that you didn't see it." Ron appreciated her concern for him. "They're all at the hospital now," he informed her. "I was hoping maybe we could go get a drink somewhere and relax after all the stress."

"I'm sorry Ron, but Rachel asked me to stay here and be with Shawn after everything he's been through." Rebecca felt torn, but she had made a promise to Rachel.

"Are you kidding?" His attitude changed quickly to bewilderment and anger. "He didn't even go to the hospital with Tanner?"

"No, I'm not kidding. This is a pretty big thing for a young man his age to go through with his dad, especially with the extreme fears he is already tormented by." Rebecca was irritated with him as well for not being sympathetic to Shawn's feelings.

"This is insane! Someone needs to kick this boy's butt and tell him to grow up. You're all just making his problem worse. His dad is going to need his help now more than ever." He was furious.

"Ron, this isn't that kind of problem. You can't just whip him into shape," her tone lightened in an attempt to keep him calm, knowing he just didn't understand the situation. She didn't want him upset with her or Shawn. Most of all, she didn't want trouble between Ron and Tanner. This was Tanner's brother and if Ron made a division over Shawn, Tanner would make Ron leave.

"You're all crazy. You can give me a call when you're done babysitting," he turned around and stormed off.

119

Rebecca hated Ron being mad at her. However, her friendship with Rachel had been important to her since they were kids. There was no debate in her mind where her devotion would lie if he pushed her.

Rebecca figured everyone would be hungry later. Before it went bad, she quickly put away the food Victoria and Rachel had prepared for dinner. Then she headed for Shawn's room. Once there, she knocked on the door. There was no answer, which didn't surprise her.

"Shawn, it's Rebecca. You and I are pretty much the only ones in the house. I was hoping you'd keep me company." She tried to persuade him to come out.

No reply. Not a sound she could hear.

"I'm sorry about your dad, that must have been horrible for you to go through. Do you want to talk about it?" she asked, knowing he could hear her.

"No!" he answered quickly and firmly.

"Okay, no problem. Will you let me in though? I feel stupid talking to a door," she said.

He opened the door to the darkened room.

"Wow, it's gloomy in here," Rebecca complained.

"Yeah, I like it that way," he mumbled, lying on his bed and staring at his iPad.

"Rachel used to do the same thing," she told him, as she went over and turned on the little lamp on his desk. "She did it whenever she was depressed. She thought it made her feel better, but it actually made her feel worse."

He watched her closely, surprised that she presumed to just make herself at home and turn on his light. He shielded his eyes from the glare but didn't reply.

"I heard you were really there for your dad today." She took a seat on the chair by his desk.

"Yeah, well, I couldn't even get myself to go to the hospital when the ambulance took him away," he snapped, furious with himself.

"So what?"

"It's my dad. I should be there for him."

"You were. You're judging yourself way too harshly."

"How do you figure? My dad might die and I'm here," he debated.

"I don't think you really believe he's going to die. Tanner said the EMT thought your dad would be okay. I think if you really believed your dad might die, you'd be at the hospital. You were focused on your dad the whole time he was stuck and the minute you heard he might be okay, your mind got focused back on your panic attacks," she reasoned.

"That doesn't make me feel any better about myself," he argued, despite knowing she was right.

"Shawn, it should. You made a big step today. You just need to realize it. You went outside and did all those things with no panic attacks at all. It shows that if you don't fear the attacks you can make them go away. Today proved that."

"I wish I could believe that," he said. He had never thought of it that way before. The fact that he didn't have any attacks and he was outside all that time made him think.

"You can, I'll prove it." She was ready for the challenge.

"What do you mean? How can you prove it?" He looked confused but was willing to let her try. He needed hope right now.

She stood up. "Get up," she grabbed one of his hands, pulling him up off the bed. "Follow me." She pulled him behind her, hurrying out of his room, but not before clicking on the wall light to his bedroom as she passed. Another one of her stubborn moves to help him make steps to get out of depression. She wanted his room lit up, not dark.

"What are you doing?" he asked, but he couldn't help but let out with a slight laugh, enjoying her playful side. He had no idea what she was up to. From what he'd heard about her though, it could be pretty much anything.

She pulled him to the stair rails. "Race me," she told him, pointing at the left rail as she stood behind the right rail.

"You're crazy," he looked at her in disbelief. "My dad could be dying in the hospital right now. I'm not going to play on the stair rails with that happening."

"Yes you are, get up there." She put her leg over the rail, to straddling it and facing backwards. "Are you afraid that a girl might beat you?

He looked at her like she was insane for doing this right now and for thinking she could beat him. He's been doing this since he was little. He gave out with a slight chuckle then leaped on the rail and down they flew. It was a fast, smooth ride and very fun. He beat her and right away she challenged him again, giving him no time to think.

"Go again! You can't beat me twice," she raced up the steps, not waiting for his answer. He followed quickly. Down they went again, faster this time. He still beat her, but just slightly.

At the bottom of the rails she didn't dismount. She stayed sitting as if on a horse and he did the same.

"See what I mean? If you don't focus on the panic attacks and fear them then you won't have one. Instead you'll have fun," she smiled, looking up at the stair rails. "Don't let these phobias run your life, stopping you from doing the things you want to do. Don't let it keep you in a dark room, depressed. There are things you can do to make them go away. Just let the feeling come and pass you by like a wave in the sea. Don't try to run and hide from it."

Shawn looked at her intently, considering every word she said. He was building hope. Something he hadn't had in a long time. He was starting to think maybe there was a way for him to become a normal person again and have a life. Just maybe.

Her cell phone rang and their faces dropped, knowing it would be news about his dad and it could be good or bad. Rebecca answered the phone and heard Rachel's voice.

"Neil's going to be just fine," Rachel informed her. Rebecca gave Shawn thumbs up and could see the relief flow over his face. "How's Shawn?"

"Shawn is doing good. Did Neil need surgery? Will he be able to use his arm like normal again?" Rebecca wanted details.

"We'll give you all the details when we get home, we will be leaving in about 20 minutes. Shawn is all right though?" she questioned a second time.

"Yes, everything is fine here, we'll see you soon," Rebecca replied, then hung up.

"So, Dad is going to be okay," Shawn assured himself, relieved.

"Yes, he's going to be fine. Rachel and Tanner will be heading back home in about 20 minutes to give us all the details."

They started to get off the rails, but before they could totally dismount a noise came from the front door. Ron entered, catching them still on the rails. It was obvious to him that they had just been having fun together sliding down the rails. Disbelief and anger fell over his face.

Chapter 9

"You couldn't go to the hospital with your brother, but you can play games in here with my girlfriend?" Ron stood tall and outraged in the doorway.

"Ron! That was uncalled for!" Rebecca snapped at him, furious, as both of her feet hit the floor. "This was my idea not his!"

Shawn looked crushed. He was embarrassed at Ron's accusations regarding his girlfriend and he was ashamed that he wasn't there with his father. His face went red and he felt guilty, as if he had just committed a serious sin. He ran up the stairs to his room as fast as his legs would take him.

"What is wrong with you?" Rebecca stormed over to Ron, finally losing all patience with him. "Every time we start to get somewhere with Shawn, you say something stupid and mean and you set him back." She knew this was really bad. This set-back could destroy all the work Rachel and Tanner have put into Shawn so far.

"You women aren't helping him. If he can be okay in the house playing, then he can be okay out of the house. He needs to toughen up. My dad taught me to swim by throwing me in the deep end of a pool and either I swam or drowned. You better believe it taught me to swim," he shot back at her, just as angry.

That information was new for Rebecca to hear about Ron's past but right now it didn't matter.

"I know you believe that way, Ron, but in this case you're wrong." She headed up the stairs for Shawn's room. She knew she'd get nowhere fighting with Ron at the moment. He wasn't about to listen. She had much bigger problems.

"Where are you going?" he snapped at her.

"Where do you think? To try to clean up your mess," she jabbed, keeping her back to him the whole way up the stairs. She thought it would be a waste of time trying to talk to Shawn after what just happened, but she had to try.

Ron slammed the door behind him as he left the house.

"Shawn?" She knocked at his door. "Shawn, ignore Ron, he doesn't understand these things. Apparently, he was brought up in a very bad, hardcore environment, and was taught how to deal with problems through a 'tough love' philosophy. His way isn't the right way. He'll learn that as time goes on, but for now please ignore what he said. He really is a great guy, he just doesn't know any better," she pleaded through the closed door.

"He's right and you know it. I should be there with my dad right now." His voice was low and sad. "Please just leave me alone. I don't want to talk anymore." He was frustrated and ashamed. He sounded like he was on the verge of tears. She decided to take her leave, not wanting to push him to that degree.

"Okay Shawn, but I'll be right here if you do want to talk or just want some company." She hated leaving him in this state of mind. She went downstairs, frustrated because she had both Shawn and Ron to worry about now. Neither were in the right frame of mind.

Great, how can everything go wrong in such a short period of time. Here I just got done telling Rachel Shawn was okay and now she is going to come home to this mess. She was so angry with Ron she didn't even want to go outside to look for him, but she knew she had to or there'd be more trouble when Tanner got home. If Ron shot off his temper like this to Tanner, things wouldn't go well. She needed to try to get through to Ron but she wasn't sure how.

The sun was going down which didn't leave much time for Ron's outside jobs. Rebecca found him on a tractor moving sand. She didn't know what the sand was for but she didn't care. She climbed up on the tractor and stood next to his seat, hanging on as he drove around. She talked with him for a good half hour before he finally promised to try to be more understanding and quit making Shawn feel bad. She believed that he would try but she could tell he still didn't agree with any of their philosophies.

She hurried back to the main house before Rachel could get home. She wanted to be there when she arrived to fill her in on what had happened with Shawn while she was away. She was hoping that Rachel could take care of the problem without Tanner finding out.

Tanner and Rachel got home later than they expected. It was dark before they came in the front door. Tanner hustled back outside again once he changed into some work clothes. He knew there was much cleaning and disinfecting to be done after the injury, whether it was dark or not. This was an important time of year; he couldn't let things slide. The workers needed to keep working to prepare for the harvest. Neil wasn't going to be around for a few days. It was Tanner who'd have to fill in for his absence and make sure everything was still on track. He also needed to inform the staff that Neil was going to be okay. They were all very close to his family and that information would be important to them.

The minute she came in the door, Rebecca pulled Rachel aside to inform her about what had happened with Shawn and Ron.

"Everything was going well and he was having so much fun, but Ron being angry with him and saying what he did really upset him. He won't even talk to me now," Rebecca admitted, feeling like she had let her friend down.

"It's not your fault, Rebecca," she assured her. "Don't blame yourself." Her face dropped and she headed up the stairs slowly, as if trying to collect her thoughts for how she was going to handle the situation. It felt as if all her work may be down the drain now.

Once Rachel got to the top of the stairs, she looked at the crack under Shawn's door to see if his light was on. It would tell her his state of mind if the lights were off. As she suspected, they were off again which was a bad sign. She let out a sigh of disappointment and knocked on the door.

"Shawn, it's Rachel. Can I come in?"

There was a moment of silence before he responded.

"I would rather you didn't," his voice was sad and sounded off. Was he crying, she wondered? It broke her heart just to hear him that sad. His words made it clear he was giving up all hope.

"Please Shawn, I need to talk to you," she pleaded.

There was silence.

"Shawn, please," she repeated, with a more serious tone. Shawn wondered if she had news about his father and that's when the door handle turned. The door only opened about two inches before he returned to the security of his bed. The room was dark except for a small night light. It was going to be hard for Rachel to read his thoughts when she couldn't see his facial expressions clearly. It didn't matter, right now he needed the darkness. He was in a dark state of mind. What he didn't know was that it was about to get a lot darker before the light.

"Shawn." She came closer, sat on his bed, and leaned her back against the wall. She wanted to be close to him. "I know where you are right now. I've been there."

"What do you mean?" He was fighting to keep from breaking down into tears.

"These extreme fears and feelings you're having, I've had them, I've been there. I still go there at times," she reached out, touching his arm.

"I don't think so," he argued, feeling as if no one could understand the extend of these horrible feelings. He began to sob. He couldn't hold it in any longer. "I hate life Rachel; I just want to die all the time. I can't live like a normal person. I can't go outside, I can't be normal, and I'm ruining everyone else's lives." His hands flew up onto his forehead as his stress mounted.

"How do you feel you're ruining everyone's lives?" Rachel questioned gently; glad he was opening up.

"Like my parents, for instance. Do they really think I don't know they sleep in separate rooms now? Even Rebecca and Ron are fighting now because of me. I'm terrified all the time from all these horrible feelings I have and I'm losing my mind," he confessed.

"First of all, don't worry about your parents, they've been doing better now. Rebecca and Ron always bicker over everything, that's their way, they'll be fine. What is important is for you to know you're not losing your mind, trust me. It just feels like it because you don't know what's going on with your body and thoughts. I've gone through the same type of feelings in the past." She moved closer to him, rubbing his back with one hand.

"When?" He pulled his hands away from his forehead to look at her. He wanted so badly to believe her. He felt very alone with these uncontrolled feelings and state of mind.

"It started when I was 11 and my mother died. I fell apart when she died. All that was left of our family was me and my sister. My dad had left before we were old enough to know him. At first, my sister and I would fight. She didn't know anything about raising a child, she was only 19 years old. She was a sister to me, not a mom. I didn't like her bossing me around. It didn't matter if she was doing it correctly or not. In my mind, she wasn't my mom and I wanted my mom back. As I grew older, that confused state of mind and stress brought on panic attacks. That's what you're having now when you have those horrible feelings. They're called panic attacks.

"No, they're not! I've seen people have panic attacks and they're not like this," Shawn disagreed, feeling his problem was far worse.

"I'm sure the ones you saw probably weren't like yours. They were probably small ones and yours are much larger. Mine started out where I'd just get a stomach ache. But they grew to where my chest would get tight and I'd feel like I was having trouble breathing. From there it progressed into shakes and sweats."

He was surprised to hear that she had such bad panic attacks in the past. But still, he felt that his were different.

"I don't feel like I'm having trouble breathing when I have an attack, I *am* having trouble," he challenged bitterly. "My breathing problems are real, not part of my imagination."

"You're right and at the same time you're wrong. When another person has a panic attack, you can tell that they're breathing wrong. They breathe fast, short breaths through their chest instead of their stomach. They feel short of breath because they are actually starting to hyperventilate. If they'd slow their breathing down and breathe through their stomach, then they wouldn't hyperventilate, feel dizzy, or feel like they can't breathe," she explained. She was getting his attention now. If she had any idea how to control this problem, he was anxious to hear it.

"Once I started having panic attacks," she continued, "it scared me to have another and the worry brought on more. I actually got so bad that when I looked at people and objects, I felt like I was in a science fiction movie. Everyone and everything seemed to be moving slightly and I wasn't. It was the freakiest, scariest thing in the world. I knew people had no clue what I was feeling. Everyone would just tell me I was okay and for me not to worry so much. 'Relax,' they'd tell me. I'd get so mad. How could anyone relax when they feel that way?"

"I've heard those same comments from people myself, it makes me want to vomit," Shawn commented bitterly.

"Well, it doesn't work that way does it?" she questioned him.

"No, it doesn't," he replied.

"You can't just ignore the attacks or stay distracted because they come back. Maybe it helps for a little while, but that doesn't keep them away or work all the time. Mine got worse and worse until I was terrified to go for a drive or go out the door. Finally, I couldn't even leave the couch in my house. Yours is your bed. Mine was my couch."

He couldn't believe it, she really did have the same feelings he was having. Maybe slightly different, but she was definitely on the same page with his feelings. He sat up, turning towards her, wanting to hear more.

"My big sister Beth and the doctors all said the same thing, I was 'fine, just anxious,' but that didn't help me at all."

"I've been told that over and over from doctors and family," Shawn related.

Rachel stared at her fidgeting fingers as she always did when she was tense. Thinking back to these uncomfortable times wasn't pleasant. "Finally, a doctor suggested a psychiatrist. I went to a few different ones and it was no help. All they did was want to discuss my whole past since I was a toddler. It wasn't doing anything to help stop the attacks. I'm not against psychiatrists because some do a lot of good, just for me it didn't help. I think it has a lot to do with finding the right one for the right person."

"I know, I totally agree. What did you do to get rid of the attacks?" he asked, anxious for a quick cure.

"First of all, you can get rid of the attacks but it's a training you'll have to apply the rest of your life to keep them away."

"Great!" He instantly got discouraged.

"No, don't be like that, it's okay as long as you learn how to control it, instead of letting it control you," she said as she poked his chest gently. "Instead of *it* controlling *you*, did you hear that part?"

He gave her a slight grin.

"I finally ended up with agoraphobia. Basically, my phobias grew until I ended up terrified of going anywhere. It was bad. I used to want to die, just like you said, because I didn't know how to make myself feel better. I wanted to take trips and have fun like everyone else, but I couldn't."

"That's what I probably have too," he related. Everything she described sounded familiar.

"As time passed, I was finally introduced to the right therapist for me, one that did connect with me. He trained me how to deal with my panic attacks and I had a life again. Sure, I'm terrified to fly on a plane, and I may have a panic attack now and then, but I can usually control them and get where I want to go and have a great time when I do. After all, I went on an air balloon," she boasted. "I've learned it's normal to experience fear, it's just not normal when we react to things like our life is in danger when it's not. Our warning system in our bodies has turned itself up to a high level and we have to bring it down to a normal level again."

"I've never thought of it that way before. That's exciting news for me, except for the part where you said I'll have to deal with this my whole life."

"Are you kidding? Everyone in the world has their own health issues to deal with. Some people are allergic to nuts, some have asthma, diabetes, claustrophobia, back problems, knee problems, even phobia of spiders. Everyone has something. Ours happens to be panic attacks. Just like everything else in life, you'll learn how to deal with it and how to control it. You can still have a normal, happy life."

"That's a good point, I've never thought of it that way before. Well then, how do I control it?" he asked.

"First, it would be very helpful to know why the panic attacks started. Many phobic people, and trust me there are millions of them out there, were set off by some major event whether it be a sickness, accident, or something traumatic that happened in their life. Knowing what set off your attack is important. It's not a must, but I believe it helps you recover quicker."

Rachel had a good idea what started his attacks, now that his parents had told her that two of his friends had been killed. He needed to open up and really talk about it. Really let out what he has been feeling and holding in after their death.

"Really?"

"Really. It helps you to understand why this started happening to you in the first place and why it's getting worse." She took his hands in hers and looked into his eyes the best she could in the dark room. "Shawn, this won't be easy for you but you need to tell me what happened to set this off, if you know. When did you first start having these feelings? Think back."

He got quiet and paused, looking down in his lap to think. It didn't look to Rachel like he was trying to figure out what had caused it. It looked more like he knew and was deciding whether he was going to tell her or not.

There's got to be more to this story that he's holding in. He looked up to meet her eyes again as if to see if he should trust her. She waited patiently, giving him all the time he needed.

"I used to play football in the past," he started, but turned his face away from her and back to his lap. "I was pretty good at it and my girlfriend came to all my games." He paused again for a good two minutes as if deciding whether he should or even could go on.

He turned and looked at something on his computer desk.

The little box! He's got to be looking at the little box. I knew that box had to be important somehow. Rachel was extremely curious.

He put one foot on the ground and slowly the other followed. He acted as if he were actually frightened to walk over and get the box. Once he did, he got back on the bed and just looked at it as he held it in his hand. Rachel waited patiently once more, giving him the time he needed to deal with each step. It took some time, but finally he opened the box. Inside was a black ring box. He slowly opened it revealing an engagement ring. Rachel was stunned. She would have guessed a bracelet or earrings might be in the box but not an engagement ring. That item alone told her the story was going to be a bad one. She couldn't tell the colors of the ring in the dim lighting, but she knew what it looked like.

"An engagement ring," she said in a hushed tone. She figured he would have been 16 years old if this had happened a year ago when his attacks began. It had to be his first love, a very serious time in a young man's life. She awaited his explanation.

Tears filled his eyes and she wanted badly just to hold him but she didn't want to do anything to throw him off from telling his story.

"Her name was Tess," he paused, "we were in love." He paused again, having trouble swallowing because he was fighting back tears from falling. "We had been going together for a year. We talked about getting married over and over. We had our whole lives planned out: where we'd live, what kind of jobs we'd have, even how many children we'd have." He rolled the ring between his two fingers, staring at it as his thoughts flashed back and forth from past to present.

He stood back up, walked over to his desk and pulled open the top drawer. From inside, he took out a framed picture. She could see at least three other framed pictures he was keeping below that one. He looked at it painfully, yearning for his girl, then handed the photo to Rachel. It was a picture of Shawn and Tess together at one of the games. They looked very happy in the picture. He was in his team jersey and they were sitting on the bleachers. She was in jeans and a white blouse. She was stunning with long, black silky hair and she sat cuddled up in front of him. His arms wrapped around Tess the same way Tanner holds her. Tess was looking up at Shawn and he was looking down at her. The smiles on their faces and the gleam in their eyes showed their love for one another.

"She's beautiful, Shawn," Rachel expressed, feeling her own heart breaking.

He looked at her as he sat back on the bed. "We never told our parents we were that serious because they'd say we were too young to think that way. Maybe we were, but that didn't stop how we felt." He turned to look at the ring again as he continued. His voice was sad. "I was going to propose the night she was killed in a car accident. I bought her this ring. She was on the way to my game to watch me play and was killed by a drunk driver. She and her brother were both killed. They were killed on the way to see me play," he broke down sobbing. Rachel couldn't stop herself, she pulled him into her arms.

"Shawn, that wasn't your fault, it was the drunk driver's fault. That could have happened on a different day when she was driving to a movie or getting groceries for her mother. It's not because she was going to your game. Remember when I told you about the hot air balloon crashing? A sudden wind popped up and caused it to crash and the pilot nearly drowned? That wasn't the pilot's fault that happened. We paid to have him take us up in the balloon, does that mean it was our fault if he would have drowned? As sad as it is, things happen."

He sobbed and sobbed so hard that his body shook. It didn't take long before he couldn't catch his breath and went into a full-blown panic attack. Panic filled his face. "I can't breathe." He sat up, struggling, as tears flooded his face. His hands flew to his chest.

"Yes, you can breathe, Shawn." She took his hands from his chest. "Listen to me." She could see and feel the tension in his hands and body. She could tell he was about to flee. She knew the feeling of wanting to run away from the attack, but you can't, it follows you.

Shawn started to stand as if to hurry away to somewhere safe. Somewhere that would make the bad feelings stop.

"Shawn, it won't help to run," she held onto his hand, hoping he wouldn't pull away to free himself. "You can't run from it. Listen to me, I can help you."

He paused long enough to look at her hand, deciding whether to jerk free or listen.

"Stay, don't leave," she gently pulled on his hand, hoping to get him to sit again.

He sat back down to give her a chance to help, hoping for a magical quick cure. He sat at the edge of the bed, apprehensive.

His breathing was fast as he struggled for a deep breath.

"Let's slow your breathing down first thing," she spoke calmly. "Don't try to take such deep, fast breaths. Just try to take slow, full breaths. Nice and slow," she repeated, showing him as she exaggerated her own breathing pattern.

He slowed his breathing, trying to take in a slow but deep breath. He could feel a difference. His heartbeat was slowing down and he wasn't struggling as hard to get air.

"Good, now relax your muscles," she continued, touching his tight arm muscles to make him aware of how tense they were. She warned, "Don't fight the panic, let loose with your muscles like a rag doll. You can make this go away if you don't fight it. Let the panic come. Let the feelings come, it's okay. They can't hurt you."

He listened to her instructions, and he tried to relax his muscles.

"If you don't fight the attacks, they'll come and go away quickly just like a wave in the sea. Picture that, a wave, relax your body, you're in the water, feel it go past," she encouraged. She watched as he closed his eyes to actually picture a wave in the sea. She was pleased at his efforts and it was paying off as his body continued to calm.

"That's right, let the feeling come, float through it. Don't fight it," she repeated, helping him to visualize it. When she touched his arm, she could feel his muscles relax and his breathing became normal. Quickly the attack was gone.

"It worked," he looked at her in near shock. "You actually made it go away!" He acted as if she had performed a miracle.

"No, I didn't. We did. And you can even do it by yourself now that you know how," she wanted that to be clear to him. "The panic attacks started when you lost your girlfriend. When you began having them, you started to fear them which just set you into having more of them. It's a big terrible cycle. The key is learning how to not fear them and how to relax through them. The more you practice this, the less of them you'll have. You saw, it works!"

"I sure hope so, I'm counting on it," he said, weary, yet hopeful. It was as if the prison gates had opened and there was hope again.

He laid down on his bed, staring at the ceiling. He unburdened his mind, telling Rachel more about Tess. He explained how his parents knew he was devastated when she died but they had no idea to what degree he truly was affected. They did send him to doctors for depression, trying to help him, but it didn't help.

"It's just like anything else, it takes time to find the right doctor with the right treatment for each illness. I'm really sorry about Tess though, Shawn."

"Thanks, it was really good to actually tell someone about her," he admitted, as he sat up and closed the box. He then stepped over to his desk, delicately putting it back in the original spot.

She stood up, trying not to overstay her welcome, but she felt she needed to add something important to their conversation. She turned to look at his face.

"I think you'd feel even better if you'd consider talking with your parents and letting them know all about this. They have no clue what's made you upset for this long and they've probably been blaming themselves for a long time, thinking they've done something wrong as parents," she gave him a weary look.

"I feel bad. I don't want that. They've always been awesome parents." He felt concern and guilt.

She read his face. "Don't feel guilty. Just tell them the truth about what happened. That's all they want to hear. It'll help them to understand a lot more of your feelings too."

"I'll definitely consider it."

She headed towards the door, about to leave.

"Can you help me practice those breathing and relaxation techniques again tomorrow?" he asked.

"You bet I can." She stopped and turned his way. "You're going to notice a quick change when you practice these techniques but remember, you will have ups and downs until you get past the extreme fears and get your training down."

"Well, I've been training for sports all my life. I can train for this and I can handle it," he voiced, determined.

"Okay then, let's get started with you opening these curtains during the day and turning your lights on when it's dark outside." Rachel walked over and opened the curtains to brighten the room. Shawn looked curiously at her as he squinted his eyes, not seeing what the light had to do anything.

"When you seclude yourself in a dark room you are giving in to the fear. That will be part of your practice, not giving into these desires," she explained.

"Rebecca said the same thing to me earlier," he acknowledged, realizing he'd better listen if they both suggested it. He laid back on his bed, thoroughly worn out. It had been a long, exhausting day.

"Come down and eat some dinner before you go to sleep," she encouraged. She knew he needed to get more food in him, he looked undernourished. She also didn't want him to start avoiding Ron. She felt confident that if Ron started anything, Tanner would put an end to it.

After opening up about Tess and knowing he had a way to control his thoughts and feelings, he felt relieved. Tired or not he was anxious to progress in his practice and continue to go forward. Whatever she suggested he would try to do. He wanted to feel better and be normal again.

It was clear to her that Shawn had been not only suffering from panic attacks, but he was still holding on to the loss of his girlfriend and blaming himself for her death. He had been holding a lot on his shoulders for a long time and this was a great start towards recovery. Looking at him, Rachel thought, *Tonight he just might get an actual good night's rest and that would be a good thing.*

Chapter 10

Rachel and Rebecca talked as they reheated the meal that Rebecca had put away when everyone left for the hospital.

"That explains why Shawn has been upset for such a long time," Rebecca realized after Rachel filled her in on what she and Shawn had discussed upstairs. "Now that it's out in the open, it's going to really help with his healing. That is, if Ron doesn't mess it up again. I'm really sorry about that Rachel," her voice dropped with guilt. She placed the warm lasagna on two pot holders in the center of the table.

"It's not your fault. You were just trying to watch out for Shawn like I asked. I'm sorry I caused trouble between you and Ron." She didn't like Ron's attitude with Shawn at all but she could understand why Ron reacted the way he did.

When Shawn came down for dinner, Ron acted like nothing had happened between them. Rebecca figured he must have been worried about her still being mad at him and didn't want to chance making things worse. Whatever the reason, she was glad and so was Rachel.

"Where's Mom and how's Dad?" Shawn asked Tanner.

"She stayed at the hospital with dad. You couldn't drag her away from him if you tried. The doctor said he broke his arm in two places but they didn't have to put a plate in his arm, which they thought might happen when we first arrived. The injury was bad but not as bad as we thought. A lot of that blood was because he was bleeding before someone found him," Tanner explained as he tried to update everyone on Neil's progress.

"That's good news," Ron acknowledged.

"He'll have to be watched for blood clots and go to physical therapy for a while in the future to build up his strength and muscles again, but it could have been much worse," Tanner said, his relief showing.

"It would have been much worse if you men hadn't been there to save him. All the workers are talking about what you guys did to get the bleeding stopped and get his arm out. It was amazing and I'm sure he's proud of all of you," Rebecca intervened, looking at each one of the men.

"The workers helped too; it wasn't just us. We're all one big family around here, that's for sure." Tanner was proud of the way that everyone had chipped in during the emergency to do what they could.

After they finished dinner, Ron asked Rebecca if she wanted to go to the restaurant for a night cap. She agreed and they wandered over to the restaurant. As it turned out, it was a very fancy restaurant requiring a coat and tie. Either that wasn't mandatory, or they just knew Ron was a friend of Tanner, because they didn't make him wear one. The lighting was low and the music was soft and relaxing.

"This place is really nice," Rebecca told Ron as she looked around, impressed.

"I thought you'd like it," Ron gave her a slight grin.

They strolled over to the bar, each taking a seat. Ron ordered drinks while Rebecca watched the live band. There were three couples slow dancing, but all the dining tables were empty due to the late hour.

Rebecca was hoping Ron would ask her to dance but if not, she was planning to ask him.

"They even have a dance floor," she hinted, but Ron didn't take the bait. She wasn't sure why not.

After their first drink, Ron noticed that a man caught Rebecca's eye as he walked past them towards the restroom. He looked handsome in his jacket and tie and she couldn't help but notice him. She didn't stare. It was a quick glance as she turned her attention back to Ron. He had seen her notice him, though, and felt even more out of place in his shirt and jeans now. She knew he caught her looking by his suddenly disturbed facial expression. She realized now that it was his appearance that was bothering him, in addition to his natural tendency to get jealous.

"Ron, will you dance with me?" She tried to push past his insecurities. "Please? You know I love to dance with you."

It was too late though. His romantic mood was gone.

"I'm tired. It's been a long, stressful day. I think we should go," he stood up, pulling out his wallet and leaving money on the counter.

She didn't fight it. The fact was, it had been a stressful day for everyone and maybe a good night's sleep was a good idea. Her hopes were high that tomorrow will be a better day.

***

At the hospital, Neil woke several times just long enough to feel Victoria's comforting hand in his and see her warm smile. Being sedated with all the pain medicine made it hard for him to stay awake. When he was finally able to stay awake briefly, she told him that his arm would heal and he'd be good as new in six weeks. She knew his concern would be if his arm would still be workable at his winery. He appreciated that she knew him so well and that she was there for him. He appreciated much more than that, too, and he wanted her to know.

"I've treated you horribly this year, Victoria, and here you are by my side as always," his voice was ashamed but his eyes read love and appreciation for her.

"Don't you even think about that right now. I've been acting like a fool too," she claimed, rubbing his hand, not wanting him stressed when he was already seriously injured. She was just glad he was going to be okay. "I'm sorry too, I just couldn't quit thinking about where you might have been when you were gone for those three days. Who you might have turned to for comfort rather than me," she admitted, avoiding eye contact and feeling shame for her thoughts.

"I need to think about it now, and to never let this happen between us again. As for the three days I was gone, there was no person I went to for comfort. I had a bottle of Jack Daniels and a motel bed. I felt like I let you all down, not even being able to help my own son. We were losing him and you were extremely unhappy. It's tough loving someone as much as I love you. I want you to be happy. When you were unhappy and I couldn't fix it, I was dying inside. I hadn't slept in days and I couldn't watch you any longer, that's when I left. I drove and drove until I couldn't drive anymore. I got a motel room, took my bottle of Jack Daniels and slept for 48 hours. Never even got up to eat.

I think the only reason I woke up was because Tanner called me. He didn't know I wasn't at home. He was overjoyed to inform me that he was getting married and planned on bringing his bride back to our place for a while after their honeymoon. It was the best news I'd heard in a year, to tell you the truth. I wasn't only glad he was getting married but glad he was coming home. I had high hopes that it would help change things around here. It would be something that would help with Shawn and bring you happiness at the same time. I couldn't wait to get home and tell you, but it took me all day just to drive back home again." He gave out with a slight chuckle at his own ignorance for driving that far.

"I remember when you got back home and rushed into the house to tell me. At first, I didn't even hear your words, my mind was focused on wanting to know where you were for three days. It took me a few minutes before it sank in that Tanner was getting married and coming home," she revealed to him as she thought back to that day.

"I was just being an ornery fool. I would never go to anyone other than you for comfort, Victoria," he continued. "I love you. I know my moods keep going back and forth making it hard for you to trust me, but not anymore. You're everything to me, no matter what happens with our children. I'm not whole without you. I'm sorry. I really am. Can you ever forgive me?" He squeezed her hand, wanting badly to just hold her.

"Oh Neil, of course I forgive you. You're my life, my love," she began to cry, rubbing his hand against her face and kissing it.

He lifted his good hand with all the tubes and wires hooked to it and pulled her down and kissed her. He needed to feel the warmth and passion of her lips together on his.

"Oh Neil," she cried, as she kissed him passionately.

"Victoria," he whispered as he fought back tears. He had missed their closeness and he missed her. It felt to him like they had been apart for a year and were now finally back together again. It felt wonderful.

***

The next morning, Tanner and Ron went out into the winery to work. With Neil laid up, Tanner took on a lot of responsibility. It was a good thing that Tanner had grown up working the vines and knew the business well.

Rachel and Rebecca went out first thing in the morning, roaming the winery. It was beautiful and there was so much to see. They could have walked, talked, and laughed all day together in the vineyard, but they didn't. They figured that they would walk around for an hour or so then go back inside to take over Victoria's tasks while she was at the hospital with Neil. The men were outside working hard to do their part and Shawn was inside, wishing he was outside.

Shawn stayed in his room for the first hour after breakfast. Now that he was relaxed enough to roam the house instead of staying in his room, that is exactly what he did. He wanted to feel freedom again and be near people. The problem was, there were no people around in the house. Not even the maids that come to clean every other day. He poured himself a cup of coffee then went into the front room where the checker game was set up. He fiddled with the chips for a while, thinking about how badly he wanted to be working outside with Tanner and Ron. Yet still he felt he couldn't.

He heard Rachel and Rebecca's voices in his head. *Control the fear, don't let the fear control your life.* He fought with thoughts over and over before walking to the front door. His steps were small. When he finally reached the front door he just stood there for a while, trying to convince himself to open it. Finally, he opened the door. Just a crack, just to look out. He couldn't really see much and when nothing seemed to happen, he opened the door a little further. As he peered around it, he could see the beautiful vines and grapes that he normally only saw from a distance through his bedroom window. They looked fresh, beautiful, and inviting. He was desperate to walk over to them and eat a grape as he did when he was a young boy, when he had no worries.

He could feel the adrenaline start to shoot through his body and he didn't know if it was just the fear of an attack or if an actual attack might be heading his way. He backed into the house and shut the door, trying to calm himself. Again, he heard the words in his head. *Control the fear, don't let the fear control your life. Don't be afraid of the feelings, let them come, they can't hurt you.* Irritated with himself for closing the door, he opened it once more. He stood with the door open as he practiced his relaxation. *Relax the muscles,"* he lectured himself, loosening his arms and shoulders. *Breathe slow, deep breaths, not short, fast ones.* He was surprised, it was helping.

He opened the door wider and took a step out. He stopped outside the door and just stood there, looking around the winery. It felt good. He could feel the warmth of the sun beating down on his face and he could smell the fresh air. It felt great. He slowly went down to the bottom of the steps, then stopped. He couldn't believe he had made it that far without a panic attack. *Baby steps,* he reminded himself, then went back inside after another minute, not wanting to push things too far.

Rachel and Rebecca were in one of the fields tasting grapes off the vines while Rachel explained the different varieties that she had learned about from Tanner and Neil. As Rachel talked, she had noticed that Shawn was stepping out the front door of the house. She couldn't believe it and nudged Rebecca to look. She was glad they were far off and to the side where Shawn couldn't see them watching.

"He's actually out the door, looking around," Rachel had announced, surprised. "He's all on his own."

"It's good he's alone. He won't feel the pressure of anyone pushing him," Rebecca observed. They had watched as he slowly worked his way to the bottom of the steps. He had stopped at the bottom, just taking in the fresh air for a few minutes before returning inside.

Rachel grabbed Rebecca, "This is great!" she said, thrilled at his progress. She of all people knew what big steps these were. "He's terrified to go outside, for him to do it without any emergency or distraction is excellent."

"He's doing really well," Rebecca agreed, happy for him and for her friend who was putting all her effort into helping him.

"I have to tell Tanner, come on." She hurried for the building where she had last seen Tanner and Ron working. They were doing their final checks on all of the tractors, getting ready for the harvest. They had to make sure nothing went wrong with any of the tractors when the grapes were ready to be picked. That's what Neil was trying to accomplish when he was hurt. One of the big tractors had been locking up and when he found the problem and tried to clear it on his own, his arm got stuck inside.

"Tanner," Rachel called out as she ran into the building. Tanner and Ron had their heads inside an engine, working.

"What's wrong," Tanner lifted his head, turning quickly towards Rachel. He had just handled a recent emergency with his dad, his guard was up.

"Nothing, that's just it, nothing," she ran up to him, eager to tell him everything. Rebecca moved over next to Ron as he watched both women curiously.

"Shawn came out of the house all the way down the steps on his own. All alone. We saw him from the field," she described, slightly out of breath. Tanner had a big smile across his face for his brother's progress until Ron commented.

"Is that all? What's the big deal? He was outside the other day helping with his dad," Ron said with an irritated tone as he turned away from the women. He grabbed a cloth from the workbench to wipe the black grease off his hands. Rebecca followed him, reminding him of his promise to take it easy on Shawn.

"I'm sorry, but him going out the door a couple of steps is not a big deal to me and it shouldn't be to you. The guy knows how to walk, he's not a baby. I think you women are ridiculous."

"It is a big deal," Rachel snapped at Ron after overhearing his comment to Rebecca.

"Yeah, whatever you say," he wiped his hands, looking away from her.

"It's a good thing, hon," Tanner told Rachel, trying to get her attention away from Ron. His hands were black with grease so he couldn't put his arms around her. "I'm really happy to hear it," he told her. "I have to finish up here, but we'll talk more about it later." He tried postponing their discussion, knowing if they spoke more about it in front of Ron it would just cause problems and upset Rachel.

Rachel could see Rebecca whispering to Ron and trying to reason with him but getting nowhere. It was obvious he objected to how they were handling things with Shawn.

Rachel understood Tanner's unspoken message and the women quickly took their leave, heading for the main house.

"I don't know why Ron keeps being such a jerk when it comes to Shawn," Rachel said bitterly as she stomped forward.

"He's got dark shadows following him around from his own past," Rebecca tried to reason.

"What do you mean?" Rachel didn't know much about Ron's past. She had always been focused on Tanner and helping her aunt. Aunt Flora and Harvey had given her warnings of Ron being rough around the edges, but they also said he was a good guy. She had also been warned about his dad being bad news, but she never pursued the reasons as to why he was bad news. She felt a little guilty for not finding out more about Ron, with him being such a close friend and all.

"I just know things. He's recently told me little things that give me strong clues that we need to have just as much understanding and patience with him as we do Shawn," she came to Ron's defense.

"Really?" Rachel looked at her friend, seeing the concern in her face. Ron was someone Rebecca cared for a lot and he was hurting too, apparently. "I'm sorry Rebecca, I didn't realize. I'll try to remember that and be more patient with him." They quickly stopped their conversation as they entered the main house, not wanting others to hear.

Meanwhile, Tanner and Ron were still working on the machinery in the big shed.

"Why do you let these women keep coddling your brother? He was out here helping like a man the other day, acting totally normal. Then, when they coddled him, he went back to being an invalid," Ron told Tanner, bothered.

"Ron, you don't understand, you've probably never had a panic attack in your life." Tanner tried to be patient with him as he grabbed for another tool.

"Yes, I have," he snapped, standing up tall to show he was serious and knew what he was talking about.

"What? When?" Tanner paused his work to challenge him.

"Many times, after my mom…" he paused then started again. "When I was 12, my dad started getting drunk and turning mean. It sent me into my first panic attack. I hyperventilated so bad I nearly fainted."

"Well that sounds awful, all right," Tanner softened. "You said it was your first, what happened after that one?" Tanner was curious, trying to hear out his friend and see where he had gotten his harsh perspective on treating panic attacks.

"When I tried to talk to my dad about the feelings I was having he was always drunk and didn't want to hear it. He told me to get to work and he'd throw my butt out on the store floor. Sometimes after an attack I'd be scared, in my room, crying. He would find me and yell, 'Quit being a cry baby. Here, I'll give you something real to cry about.' Then he'd beat me with his belt. Afterwards he would add, 'Apparently, you have too much time on your hands if this is all you can think about.' Then he'd throw me back in the store to work some more. I was so afraid of him giving me more beatings, I wasn't focused on my attacks anymore," he explained, "and they went away."

"So, you're telling me I should beat my little brother and that would help him?" Tanner questioned sarcastically as he returned to working on the tractor engine again.

"No, but if you didn't baby him and just made him get out here and work, he'd forget about those panic attacks."

"I understand what you're trying to say Ron. You feel that working distractions will make his panic attacks go away. From what I'm learning, distraction can help at times, but it can't keep them away. He has to learn how to handle them." Tanner tried once more to be patient as he reasoned with Ron.

"Did you get that from DOCTOR Rachel?" Ron said with a sneer.

"That's it!" Tanner slammed his tool down on the tractor hood, stopping his work. His patience was wearing thin. He stood up to look Ron straight in the eyes. "I suggest that you not say anything against my wife, Ron," he warned. "And you don't want to make her feel bad again like you just did. She's my wife and Shawn is my brother. I appreciate your concern for him, but your past is not an example of how I feel people with phobias should be treated. I'm sorry you had it so rough, I really am, but I don't believe in that kind of 'tough love.' I rather take Rachel's advice on how to handle Shawn. She's been there before and has gotten help from real therapists. Also, in case you didn't notice, your own girlfriend feels the same way as Rachel does. Not to mention, they both have gotten farther with him in the shortest period of time than anyone else has in a whole year."

Tanner liked Ron. Ron was actually his closest friend and he didn't want him to leave, but if he didn't back off on his attitude with Shawn and Rachel, it would come to that. "Now, do you want to hold this right here for me?" Tanner picked up his tool, pointing to a hose he was planning to clamp off in the engine. "Or do you want to keep wasting time arguing?"

Ron paused, irritated, as he thought a minute about his choices. Reaching over, Ron grabbed the tool and ended the debate. Tanner hoped that what he said to Ron would sink in this time and there'd be no more problems with him, but he wasn't convinced.

***

The next day, Neil came home from the hospital. He was happy to be home and everyone was happy to see him. His arm was covered in thick bandages and a removable cast and the whole thing was suspended in a brace.

"The doctor said he was really fortunate because his injuries were only below the elbow," Victoria informed everyone. "He'll be out of the cast in six weeks, then he'll probably need a little therapy, but they said he'd be as good as new."

"I'm so glad, Dad," Shawn told him, bringing him the newspaper. Neil was very old fashioned when it came to his morning paper. He didn't want to read it on a computer, he wanted it firmly in his hands.

It was lunch time and everyone had gathered in the kitchen, always the family's favorite hangout for food, drinks and gab.

"Thanks son, you know what I like," he took the paper, smiling up at Shawn. "Your mother will help fold the pages over so I can read it in a few minutes. I want to talk to Tanner first." He turned his attention to Tanner.

"How's the winery been doing while I've been gone the last couple days?" Neil asked.

"Just fine, Dad. Ron and I have been keeping up on everything and getting the trucks and equipment in gear for the big day. Matter of fact, things are going so well, I was thinking Ron and I might take tomorrow morning off and take the women bike riding for an outing before the harvest hits," Tanner suggested. It was more of a question than a statement, he was hoping his dad would think his idea was sound. Tanner wanted to break the tension that was going on with his friends and let everyone have a break.

"Sounds like a good plan to me," Neil squeezed Victoria's hand, showing that he knew how important it was to give time to your wife. She had been glued to his side ever since the accident and he didn't want her to leave. Tanner was relieved to see that his parents had worked things out.

Rachel and Rebecca looked at the men in surprise with smiles on their faces. They had known nothing about these plans to spend the day together, but they did know they were ready for it. Shawn, however, looked disturbed.

Rachel could tell it was a look of disappointment. She knew he also wanted to go but just wasn't ready.

Later that night, when Shawn headed upstairs, Rachel whispered to him, "You'll be going on bike trips again soon." He looked at her with doubt but at the same time with a spark of hope. If she felt that he would be doing it soon, there was a possibility that someday he might.

Tanner and Rachel sat by the fireplace with his parents, discussing the different wines that Neil and Tanner planned to make. Meanwhile, Ron and Rebecca slipped outside for an evening stroll.

Rebecca had hopes that it would be a romantic walk including looking at the stars which was one of her very favorite things to do. The fields of grapevines added to the view, along with the pretty lights that surrounded the winery gardens.

"It's so beautiful here." Rebecca leaned in close to Ron as they started their stroll through the winery with his arm around her.

"It is," he agreed with a content look.

"I could stay here forever," she claimed. She felt like the whole place was a big vacation lodge.

"I'm glad to hear that since I will be working and living here for some time," he replied. He had been missing her ever since she left Florida.

"That is, if you can let go of your problems with Shawn," she added with concern.

"What's that mean?" His tone quickly turned to irritation the minute this subject came up.

They stopped walking as Rebecca turned to face him.

"There's no way things are going to go well between you and Tanner if there is friction between you, his wife and his brother," she warned. She hated ruining their romantic walk but somehow she had to keep him from getting himself kicked off the premises.

He dropped his arm from her shoulders. "I'm just trying to help. Their way isn't working."

"How do you know? There's been big changes in Shawn since Rachel got here."

"Changes, but he's not better yet is he? Maybe in another year he might be able to walk across the street from his house to the grapes," he challenged, waving his hand towards the road.

It was hard for her, but Rebecca tried to be patient, remembering that Ron is a great guy, he was just brought up in a whole different way of life and doesn't get it.

"Ron, these attacks he has are not just a mild panic attack. These are bad! Like a horrible attack on his body and mind. If you were to see one, then you'd realize that your 'tough love' philosophy to force them away by punishment or distractions won't work. This is something that requires medication or training to control and work through. He won't take the medicine and we're not going to force it down his throat," she scrunched her eyebrows, annoyed at the thought. "It has to be done through training." She paused and looked into his eyes, hoping he'd see her point. "I know you were brought up differently, but I really need to get through to you how important this is to me. You need to back off of Shawn and try to be understanding." Her eyes pleaded with him as she rubbed her hand gently down his arm until she weaved her fingers with his.

He was torn. Now she had touched a nerve. He had his own dark shadows from his past that he was dealing with and keeping from her. It was killing him inside not to discuss them with her, but he felt that he had no choice; he'd lose her if she knew. This pressure with Shawn was just adding to it. He continued to think without a response for such a long time that Rebecca was about to ask him what was on his mind, then he came out with it.

"You don't know anything about my past and I don't want you to." He couldn't help but let out with some of his own pain as he tried to decide what else to say or reveal to her. "It's not pretty. I've learned the hard way but I'll admit that doesn't mean it was the right way. There was a lot of misery and trouble that came with that way of life." His eyes showed his own pain and she felt for him.

"Ron." She reached up, gently rubbing her fingertips across the mysterious scar that sat above his left eye. She couldn't help but feel that his secret past would explain that scar. She yearned for answers to the mysteries that came with this man she had grown so close to.

He took her hand away from the scar, giving her fingers a gentle kiss.

"There's a tough love going on between us, you know," he kept his eyes focused on her hands for the moment, as if he couldn't say what he was feeling if he looked up at her face. "One that gives me feelings I never thought I would have. Feelings that make me want to make changes; changes I never expected to make." He finally looked up and peered deeply into her eyes as if to touch her deepest thoughts.

"You're worth it," he assured her. "I'll try harder with Shawn, I promise." He couldn't believe what was coming out of his mouth, but he knew deep down that she could talk him into anything if she wanted to. He also knew that she was a smart woman. If she felt what was going on with Shawn was different, then maybe it was different and he needed to back off.

He pulled her arms around his waist and he wrapped his arms around her shoulders. Relief filled her body as she heard a different tone when he spoke this time. What he was saying worried her, to a degree. How broken was he? She knew that she would need to get him to open up about his past, but not tonight. His past would be hanging over both of them like a dark cloud until they could face it together. At the moment, she really hoped she had gotten through to him because she had fallen for him as well and she didn't want him to leave.

Chapter 11

The next day, they went to the bike trail Shawn had suggested and it was perfect. The trail went through the trees and up and down hills with all kinds of challenging terrain. They rode their bikes for a couple of hours, laughing and joking with one another then stopped for a picnic.

"Hey, Tanner?" Rebecca sat on the blanket next to Ron eating her turkey sandwich.

"What's up, Rebecca?" Tanner was ready for anything, coming from Rebecca.

"I can't help but notice that fancy restaurant you have at your winery," she had a sly smile. "Do you have connections where Rachel and I could go in the kitchen one day to see the chef cooking?" Rebecca loved cooking shows. She and Rachel used to watch them at night when they were roommates. Rachel was slightly embarrassed that her friend was being so forward, but deep down she agreed that it would be an awesome sight.

Tanner grinned as he shot a glance at Ron. They were always getting a kick out of these two women. Ron raised an eyebrow, showing Tanner he caught the look and was enjoying the discussion as well.

"I think it could be arranged at some point," Tanner replied, not committing to a set day or time. His schedule was very full already.

"That would be awesome!" Rebecca was overjoyed, shooting Rachel a smile. Rachel smiled back, thrilled at the idea of watching a chef cook in a bustling kitchen.

Tanner observed Rachel's excitement as well, which gave him the resolve to make it happen before Rebecca's return to the university.

After their lunch, Ron and Rebecca took off on a separate trail. Rebecca wanted to race against Ron and go crazy while Tanner and Rachel were ready to take it easy on the calmer trails. They liked just taking their time and enjoying the scenery whereas Rebecca's wild side needed to let out some of her energy.

"I take it there are jumps on the trail ahead?" Rachel questioned Tanner after she looked into the distance and saw what looked like Rebecca flying in the air on her bike.

"If there's not I'm sure Rebecca made one," he said, laughing when he saw Rebecca in the air.

They could hear Rebecca screaming in fun and Ron chasing after her on his bike. He yelled something antagonizing to her as he passed her up. Rachel and Tanner laughed as they watched the couple disappear into the trails as they competed against one another.

After another 45 minutes of fun, they all met up and were ready to leave. It was 3:00 p.m. and Tanner wanted to head back to the winery. He wanted to make sure they got back in plenty of time to get some work done. He didn't want his dad to be worried that things weren't getting done while he was laid up.

After the day's bike ride, Ron and Rebecca came to the conclusion that Ron could ride a bike a lot faster than Rebecca, but she could jump her bike a lot higher.

"At one spot she had her bike in the air so high and long I didn't think she was going to land on the ground again," Ron joked, amazed with her.

Rachel and Rebecca were ready for some rest after riding for that long. It was a good morning and they had a great time together. The four of them always did. That's why Tanner hoped Ron would let go of this issue he had with Shawn so it wouldn't cause problems between all of them.

After they returned, Tanner and Ron didn't even go into the main house, they just headed right into the winery. When Rebecca and Rachel entered the house, Victoria and Neil were just headed upstairs to rest. The pain pills from the hospital were making him tired and they planned to take a quick nap. Shawn was sitting on the couch looking depressed. Rebecca glanced at Rachel then she took off upstairs, knowing those two needed to talk.

"Hi Shawn," Rachel walked over and sat on the couch across from him. "That bike trail you sent us to was great."

"Yeah, it's a pretty good one," his voice was flat.

"Did you used to go there a lot with your friends?"

"All the time. But that was a long time ago," he stared at a spot on the rug, not wanting to have that discussion.

"Shawn, it's time," Rachel warned.

"What? What do you mean it's time?" He looked up at her, totally confused.

"It's time for us to practice."

"Riding my bike?" he questioned, looking at her like she was crazy.

"No silly, time for you to go outside and work through a panic attack, if you were to have one. You might not even have one but it's the only way to get past them," she encouraged.

His face went pale. It was as if she were asking him to risk his life. "I'm not ready. I can't do that," he argued, sounding angry, but at himself, not at her.

"Yes, you are ready. Shawn, I saw you walk down the steps out front. We won't go far at all. Just walk over to the vines right across the road and come back." What she was suggesting was close, yet far enough to help him feel he can actually be away from the house and survive.

"No, it'll happen, I know it will." He leaned forward on the couch and bent over, scrunching his hands together in a rough manner. Rachel thought if he had a way, he'd roll up in a ball right then.

"To be honest, it would be good if you have an attack while we're out there so you can work through it. Remember, the objective is not to run from them but to let them come and pass. Like a wave. If you feel one coming on you'll breathe through it with your stomach breathing, relax your muscles, and ride it out like I showed you the other night.

"I don't know," he stiffened up and his hands began to shake.

"Shawn, look at me." She went to his couch and sat next to him. Reaching over, she put her hands on his and squeezed them gently just as Tanner always did to help her relax and feel his support.

He turned in her direction, looking into her eyes, showing his extreme fear.

Cindi Annette

"You're already working on giving yourself a panic attack, so let's practice right now," she had to calm him down or he'd fail before they started. "Look at your hands, they're shaking." She moved her hands off his to let him see.

He watched them as they shook.

"If you want to have a normal life again you have to do the practice, just like you did with your sports a year ago. You told me you've been practicing the exercises I've taught you, just think of this as another warm-up exercise."

She could tell by his facial expression that he was thinking about everything she said and that it made sense to him. It helped him to relate to the warm-ups he did for many years.

"Now, relax your shoulders and let them drop," Rachel instructed, "like we practiced."

He did as she said and his shoulders dropped down as he released the tension.

"Now, relax your arms and shake out your hands like this," she shook her hands loosely as if to shake away the tension.

He copied each thing she did, wanting to make sure he learned it well.

"Now slow your breathing down and breathe through your stomach." As he concentrated on his breathing, she could see his shoulders start to tense up again. "Relax your shoulders and arms again and breathe slowly." He did as she instructed and his hands were no longer shaking.

"It's not easy to remember how to breathe through your stomach," he told her, but his tone was more relaxed now.

"No, it's not because all your life you've breathed through your chest. You'll get used to it but for now just try to slow your breathing down if you forget how, that's the most important thing. Many of our bad feelings come from hyperventilating when we get nervous and breathe wrong. That is why controlling our breathing is a big thing." She wanted to give him every tool she had to help him progress.

Shawn relaxed quickly. Every suggestion she gave him made a difference for the better.

"Come on Shawn, let's give it a try now," she encouraged, standing up.

He paused, not moving yet.

"You're not going empty-handed this time. You have the tools to use if you have a problem. And remember, having a problem isn't a bad thing because you'll get to practice."

He finally stood up and they headed for the front door. She opened the door and stopped as they both looked out together. His face began to pale once more.

"You're thinking about the panic attack and fearing it. Don't. Focus on your breathing and relaxing your muscles instead. We're only going to walk right over there by the vines." She pointed to the ones closest to the house. "We'll go over there and look at the grapes, maybe even taste one, then we'll come right back. We have a plan, you can do this." She stepped out the front door first, not looking back at him.

"I don't know?" he said, worried, as he crept down one step at a time following her.

"Yes, you do, let's go, don't think about it, just walk. Think about the grapes over there that we're going to taste. Try to pick from here which one you want to taste," Rachel encouraged as she continued to walk. She only hoped he was following. "You'll have to show me the ripest ones, I'm not sure how to tell them apart." She continued to talk as she headed into the roadway. "Some of the grapes are big and fat and some look small and dark. I'm not sure if the big ones or the small dark ones are the ripest." She babbled on, just praying he was still behind her. She crossed the road and was nearly to the vines now. She was hoping her comments were keeping his mind off his panic attacks and that he hadn't returned to the house.

"The big, fat, dark ones are the ripest ones," he told her as they reached the vines. Her adrenaline pumped with excitement that he was still following. His voice was music to her ears. She kept calm and nonchalant in order to keep him calm.

"Show me which ones, will you?" She wandered amongst the vines looking at all of the grapes. "Some of these are red, some are purple and some nearly black in color," she was acting lost with which one to pick. He passed in front of her and picked one, giving it to her, as he picked and ate one himself.

"Oh my, that is good," Rachel moaned. He smiled in agreement as he tasted the rich, sweet flavor in his mouth.

"These have thin skins so they'll be picked first for making Merlot," he explained, picking them each a couple more as they continued a little further into the vineyard. "We'll be harvesting soon," he added. "These grapes feel and taste ready," Shawn commented, pleased. He hadn't been out in the vineyard in a year. It felt good. Working the vines was his whole life as a child. He loved being out there and tasting the grapes.

"You can tell your dad that when you see him later tonight," she told him proudly. Shawn smiled, actually proud of himself at that moment.

"Can we walk a little farther?" he asked.

He asked! She couldn't believe it.

"Of course," she replied, pleased at his desire to continue.

They traveled down into the vines. Shawn looked around as if he hadn't seen the grapes in forever. She could tell he felt good. He felt alive again. He showed no sign of an attack and his color was great. The only problem with that was it meant he didn't get to practice. She wasn't going to depress him by mentioning that, but it did concern her. They walked back to the house and once inside, Shawn leaped around with happiness. He lifted Rachel up and twirled her around.

"I did it, I actually did it!" He acted like he'd been locked up in prison for a year and had finally been released.

"Yes, you did, you were awesome," she complimented him.

"What did you do?" Rebecca was at the top of the stairs looking down after hearing all the noise.

"I went outside. I even went across the road into the vineyard. Rachel and I ate grapes together," He ran up the stairs, lifting Rebecca in the air and twirling her as well.

"This is a great day," Shawn jumped on the rail and slid down it at full speed. Jumping feet first onto the ground he landed, looking at Rachel.

"Shawn, remember, baby steps. We still have work to do," she warned him. She was worried that he was going to get carried away and do something outside that he wasn't

167

ready for yet. He could have an attack out there and if she was not there to help him the first time, it could set him back, possibly enough that he wouldn't trust her again.

"I know. Don't worry, I'm not going to do anything stupid," he assured her. Rachel didn't feel secure with that comment. She used to say the same thing to her sister at that age, just before she did something that Beth would object to.

The next morning, Tanner woke Rachel and told her to look out the window. When she did, she saw Shawn walking around the winery property. Neither she nor Tanner could believe what they were seeing. They watched as he climbed up into the tractor seat, sitting comfortably, ready to drive it. Tanner felt that Shawn probably would have done so if he had the keys at that moment.

He strolled section to section through the vineyard checking out the grapes. He balanced on the high cement wall edges around the main winery showroom to just have some fun. He picked a flower just to smell it and enjoy the fragrance which he had not done in a year. He was one happy guy, feeling no fears.

When Tanner went downstairs, his parents were already drinking their coffee, standing together and watching Shawn through the window. His father had his good arm around his wife as they shared this special moment of happiness together. They couldn't believe their eyes. Their son was acting normal again and he was having fun.

"We saw him out there a half hour ago when we got up. Who knows how long he's actually been out there," Neil announced to Tanner, delighted. "I couldn't be a happier man, having both of my sons here enjoying themselves."

"It makes me just as happy, Dad." Tanner gave his dad a pat on the back and joined him as he looked out the window.

Rachel was pleased for Shawn and his family, but she was very worried inside. He was diving back into the world but has not had many opportunities to practice. Panic attacks don't just go away without practice. Sooner or later she knew he was going to have an attack. He was like a ticking bomb waiting to go off. She didn't know when, but it was going to happen.

Rebecca entered the kitchen, wondering what everyone was looking at.

"Take a look," Rachel told her as she went over to get herself a cup of coffee.

"That's Shawn out there," Rebecca said, stunned.

"It sure is, thanks to my wife over there," Tanner said proudly.

"It wasn't me, this is all Shawn," Rachel countered, with a little irritation in her voice. He deserved the credit for working on his problem, not her.

Rebecca turned to look at Rachel. She knew the look on Rachel's face and that her slightly agitated tone meant something was bothering her. She moved over next to her as Tanner and his parents changed the subject, getting back to their usual harvesting discussion. "What's up?" she whispered.

Rachel looked at Tanner and his parents, then down at her coffee as she poured cream into it. Stirring her coffee, she spoke quietly, not wanting the others to hear. "He hasn't dealt with a panic attack outside yet. When he has one it's not going to go well if I'm not with him the first time."

"He didn't have any issues yesterday when you were both outside tasting grapes, did he?" Rebecca poured herself a cup of coffee as she spoke.

"No, but he's pushing it too fast without practice," Rachel reached over to the counter to grab a danish.

"Then try to walk around with him today. Try to do something out of the ordinary that might set one off. Then you can be there to practice with him if he has one," Rebecca suggested as she grabbed herself a cheese danish as well.

"I agree. That's a good idea I'll do that right away," Rachel said, trying to eat quickly to get outside. She had a plan now and she felt better.

Shawn entered the kitchen. Everyone pretended they hadn't been watching him.

"Hi everyone, it's a great morning out there today," Shawn declared, all smiles as he headed for the coffee pot.

Ron entered the kitchen next.

"Hi," Rebecca turned, giving Ron a warm smile.

"Hi beautiful." He came over and gave her a quick kiss on the lips then took a bite of her danish.

"Hey, watch it now, don't be eating my danish," she teased. "Want some coffee?" she offered, ready to pour him a cup.

"Sure, thanks," he grabbed a plate and started dishing out his food. "I saw you out there walking all over this morning, Shawn. Good for you man," he said, taking a bite of the bacon from his plate.

Rebecca rolled her eyes. *So much for no one making a big deal of this or acting like they were watching him.* She was okay with it, though. At least Ron was being positive for once.

"Yeah, I feel great." Shawn joined Ron, filling a plate for himself, proud as he could be.

"I'm thinking three days, Dad, maybe four at the most." Tanner changed the subject, not wanting Shawn to feel uncomfortable with everyone staring at him.

"I can't believe the harvest is here and I'm in a cast and useless," Neil grumbled.

"Hardly useless, Dad. You can yell at everyone just as well with that cast on as you normally do without it," Tanner teased. "You've got Ron and I and all the workers to be your arm for you, just tell us what you want done."

"And me," Shawn turned around, determined to help.

Neil smiled, thrilled that Shawn was ready to help, but Tanner looked at Rachel in question. He could see the worry in her face and Tanner quickly advised, "We'll see little brother, don't rush it."

"I'm fine, Tanner, I feel fine." He was full of energy. He shoved his eggs in his mouth like it was a race to eat and get back outside.

"Why don't we give it a little test today," Tanner challenged. Rachel looked curiously at him.

"Sure, what do you have in mind?" Shawn asked eagerly.

"Let's work on my old car today and maybe practice a little driving around the property," Tanner suggested. Everyone got quiet. Rachel knew that Tanner thought he was helping her by keeping Shawn by his side and doing a simple task. She appreciated the thought, but it wasn't quite what she was after.

"Okay, you're on," Shawn accepted the challenge.

Rebecca gave Rachel an odd look and Rachel knew they had the same thought. How was she going to get to practice with him while the men are working on cars and driving? What now?

After breakfast, Ron and Neil went into the winery while Rebecca and Rachel helped Victoria clean up. Tanner and Shawn headed for the car. Rachel stood in the kitchen, watching them go out the door, not sure what she should do.

"I can't follow them out there while they are working on the car. It would be too obvious that I'm worried about leaving Shawn alone. He needs confidence, not to feel like he's being baby sat," Rachel told Rebecca.

"What's the matter? Why do you want to follow Shawn?" Victoria sounded confused.

"He's bound to have a panic attack at some point while he's outside and it would be better for Rachel to be there to help him through it the first time. If he's not prepared and has a bad attack without someone there to guide him through in a positive way, it might make him go back in that room upstairs and never want to come out. He could feel like nothing works no matter what he tries and then he'll want to give up," Rebecca explained, as they dried the dishes.

"Go out there, then," Victoria demanded of Rachel, worried for her son. "You have to be there." She had just gotten her son back and didn't want to chance anything making him go back into his depression.

"I can't just go out there now," Rachel replied, concerned. "I don't want him to feel like an invalid or that could set him back too."

"Yes, you can. Women go outside watching their men work on cars all the time. Some men, that's all they do all day is work on their cars for a hobby. The only way the women get to see them is to go in the garage while they're working," Victoria reasoned.

"I agree with Victoria. Just go out there and act like you're interested in what they're doing," Rebecca joined in. She turned Rachel around and pushed her towards the door. "We have too much invested in Shawn to let this blow up in our faces."

Victoria appreciated Rebecca's forcefulness on her friend. Rachel was used to it. Many times throughout the years as roommates and as best friends, Rebecca's pushy ways helped her through some of her own extreme fears.

Rachel went out the door, trying to plan what she'd say before arriving in the small garage where the old car was parked. She felt that this building must have been one of the first buildings ever built, besides the main house. It was small compared to the other buildings and though it was well kept, it also appeared very aged.

Tanner and Shawn had their heads under the hood of the car and Tanner was changing some spark plugs. Shawn had a spark plug in his hand and was bent over the car, watching everything Tanner was doing.

"How's it going?" Rachel asked innocently.

"Fine hon, the car is in good shape; we're just changing the spark plugs. She isn't starting right up in the morning and it's idling pretty rough. Those are pretty sure signs that she needs new spark plugs," he explained to Rachel. "Let me have the last one, Shawn, and that should do it." Tanner took the spark plug from him. "Start her up now and let's hear how she sounds." Rachel got a kick out of how Tanner called the car a 'her' and a 'she.'

Shawn moved around to the driver's door, anxious to see if the car would start up quickly.

Tanner backed away from the engine. "Okay, start her up."

Shawn started the car and the engine fired right up. He got back out of the car, leaving the engine running to go in front and hear how it was sounding.

"Started right up and sounds way better," Shawn told Tanner as he listened to the smooth engine.

"Sure does," Tanner smiled.

They fiddled with the engine a little longer, then Tanner said it was time to take it for a spin.

Before loading into the car Rachel couldn't help but tease Tanner. "Start 'her' up? See if 'she' sounds better?"

Tanner looked at her with a lifted brow, then replied, "Anytime I've worked on this car and was angry or rough, it would never start. But if I keep calm and gentle, it always starts. I figure it's got to be a female car," he teased. Shawn heard him and started busting up laughing. Rachel couldn't help but laugh too.

Rachel hopped in the back seat. Tanner was just focused on working with Shawn's driving practice. He glanced at Rachel, curious as to why she was coming, but didn't say anything. If she wanted to come along, he didn't have a problem with it. He settled into the passenger seat and Shawn got behind the wheel.

"I don't have to really tell you how to drive, you already know from driving all these trucks for years. But you do have to learn some safety rules for going out on the road. First of all, always make sure everyone in your car including yourself has a seat belt on before you ever move the car," Tanner lectured. All three of them started putting on their seat belts.

"I know Tanner, I did have drivers training a year ago, you know," Shawn said as he put his seat belt on.

"Did Mom mention that your permit might still be good?" Tanner questioned.

"Yeah, but only for a few more weeks," he sounded discouraged.

"That's okay. We'll just have to get your license before it expires," Tanner informed him optimistically. Tanner told Shawn to drive around the winery grounds for the moment to see how he does. Tanner just wanted to get the car moving before Shawn could get nervous and suddenly change his mind about learning to drive.

He backed out of the building slowly and carefully, just as he should. As he drove around the winery, he was cautious, watching out for all the guests. It was no different than when he used a tractor, so this was no challenge.

After driving around for 10 minutes, Tanner suggested, "You're doing great. I think we should go out on the street now. But before we do, I want you to practice stopping a little quicker." Tanner wanted to make sure if there were any problems on the street, Shawn would react quickly.

"If I say 'stop' then I want to make sure you stop right when I say to. Out on the street, it could mean a difference of hitting another car or even a person."

"Okay," Shawn replied.

"Now, just drive like normal," Tanner tried to act casual, not wanting Shawn to be aware of when he would order him to stop.

"Stop," Tanner ordered as he saw a squirrel starting to cross the road. It was just the right excuse for Tanner to test Shawn.

Shawn hit the brakes hard and fast. Everyone flew forward into their seat belts.

"That was a quick stop, all right," Tanner said as he started laughing. Rachel joined in, busting up in the back seat. Shawn looked at both of them.

"Well, you said to stop quick," Shawn said, sounding defensive.

"You're right, I did tell you that and you did great. Maybe next time you might not want to push quite as hard on the brakes. You want to stop quick but not so quick the car behind you crashes into the back of you or you give your passengers whiplash," he teased, sounding like the older brother Shawn was used to. Shawn started laughing too.

As they drove around, Shawn seemed relaxed and was having a great time with no signs of a panic attack. Tanner had him drive off the winery property and into the residential area. He did great. They spent a half hour driving around nearby blocks without any problems.

While Tanner and Rachel were busy with Shawn, Ron decided to take Rebecca for a ride on one of the quads.

Chapter 12

Rebecca pleaded to get to drive the quad but Ron refused to let her, claiming Tanner would kill him if he allowed it. He took her for a ride all around the winery property. There were many fields of grapes and hills to explore. The place was gorgeous and when they got to the top of one particular hillside they just sat on the quad, looking over the property. It was an amazing view and they were in awe. They could see the large wine making and storage buildings. They watched as workers went in and out of work sheds and cabins. They could see the winey guests buzzing around the winery and going into the restaurant, main store and tasting room. Rebecca pointed out the main house that sat behind it all like a watchman over a palace. There were grapevines as far as their eyes could see, making everything green and beautiful.

"Can you imagine owning all of this?" Rebecca asked Ron.

"I'm sure their families have worked hard for many generations to build this place up and make it successful." Ron admired their hard work and what they had achieved.

"I'm sure you're right," Rebecca agreed.

"I like it here. Neil is a real good man to work for. He likes things a certain way but is very good and patient with all his workers. That includes me, which is good because I know nothing about making wine," he let out with a smirk.

"I'm glad you like it here. I don't want you to leave," she gave his waist a squeeze as she sat behind him on the quad then laid her head against his back. He turned his head to look at her. She lifted her head, looking into his eyes, feeling those unspoken words that lovers feel as their lips met.

"I'm glad you don't want me to leave," he gave her a flirtatious grin.

"Let's just stay up here all day," she whispered.

"Wouldn't that be nice." He gently rubbed his hand across her cheek, then his finger across her lips, and he kissed her once more. Her warmth and passion were driving him for more, a lot more, but he knew he had commitments. "We've already been gone a long time and I'm sure Tanner and everyone else are back by now, we'd better get back too."

"I know, but you can't blame a girl for trying."

"You're a hard woman to resist Rebecca," he stated as he fought off his own desires, turning around before he gave in to them.

A sweet smile crossed her face as she felt her victory of enticing him.

He started the quad and they headed down the hill.

While driving back, Ron noticed a work truck that was stalled in one of the fields. A worker had his head over the engine, trying to see what was wrong. Ron drove up to the truck. One thing Ron was familiar with was engines.

"Do you need some help there, Juan?" Apparently, Ron was already getting to know some of the workers by name, Rebecca noticed.

"I don't know what's wrong, it just died?"

"Let's see if I can help." Ron got off the quad, glancing towards Rebecca to see if she didn't mind his stopping. She gave him an agreeable smile. She had no problem with him stopping to help someone; it revealed the tender side that he worked so hard to hide.

Later, Ron let Rebecca off at the main house and he drove the quad to put it away in the shed. Rebecca went inside to the kitchen where everyone liked to hang out. Shawn had just gotten back from his driving lesson and told Rebecca and his mother how well he did.

"Yeah, he did great out there, mom. A matter a fact, if he keeps practicing with me and gets his license, the car is his," Tanner announced, looking at Shawn proudly.

"Really, you'll give me your car?" Shawn couldn't believe it. He knew that car was always special to Tanner which made it special to Shawn. He knew that one day Tanner would let him borrow his car but he never thought he'd give it to him. Tanner loved that car.

"You bet." Tanner knew a good goal would help Shawn to continue to progress and it also made Tanner happy to bring joy to his brother when he's been so down.

"That's awesome, thanks Tanner!"

Rebecca and Victoria looked at Rachel for any sign as to whether Shawn had a panic attack or not. Rachel gave them a look that said no practice had gotten done. Their eyes showed concern even as they continued smiling, not letting Shawn know of their worries.

"I'm going to work with you and Ron tomorrow when you guys go out into the winery," Shawn announced to Tanner, feeling extremely confident. "I'm sure you guys need all the help you can get right now," he figured. He took off upstairs, skipping three steps at a time, "I'm going to text Dave and tell him I'm better," he added.

"Dave?" His mother looked surprised. "He hasn't talked to Dave in nearly a year." Rebecca and Tanner looked to Rachel for her reaction.

"Should I let him help tomorrow?" Tanner asked, not knowing whether Shawn was ready for that or not.

"You can't stop him." Rachel walked over to Tanner, looking just as concerned. "He'll lose all confidence if we stop him."

"You have to let him go," Rebecca echoed, knowing it was important as well.

"I'll practice some breathing with him tonight, but when it happens out there the first few times it can be a real blow. He'll forget every technique he's learned. Your mind just goes blank."

"What do I do if he has one?" Tanner asked, concerned.

"Think of him as me. What would you do if it were me? You always keep me calm and let me know everything is all right if I start to have a panic attack. The one thing you don't want to do is let him run back to the house. He needs to see he can survive through the panic attack while he is still outside. Meanwhile, send someone to get me."

Tanner still looked a little concerned. He didn't want to mess up and have Shawn run back home and back to depression all over again.

"You can do this Tanner; we need to work together." Rachel wanted to build Tanner's confidence. When it came to his brother, he didn't always think straight.

"I'm worried, Tanner," Victoria said, standing by the window and drying her hands on her apron. Tanner got up and went over to her, hugging his mother.

"It'll be all right mom, don't worry. You take care of Dad, we'll take care of Shawn," he promised her.

"It'll be okay, Victoria," Rebecca said, assuring her as well.

"There's a lot of us here watching out for Shawn, don't worry, he'll be all right," Rachel assured her. She understood Victoria's worry. She had gone a year with her son on the verge of suicide, acting like a total stranger to her, and now he was back. She didn't want to lose him again.

That night, Rachel went to Shawn's room to practice his breathing and relaxation with him. She warned him that an attack could hit when he least expects it, so he needs to be prepared. Shawn listened attentively to everything Rachel had to say. He wanted badly to keep progressing.

***

The next day after breakfast, the men took off to the winery. The women stayed in the kitchen and cleaned the dishes, not saying a word. Their minds were ticking away, worried about what might be happening with Shawn.

Neil went into the tasting room in the main winery building. He had to stick to light duties and not any hard labor for a while. Tanner, Ron, and Shawn went into a building that stored lots of big crates and pallets.

"Shawn, how about you get the lift then Ron and I will throw these pallets on it. I'll have you move them over to the other shed so we can make more room in here," Tanner directed Shawn as he headed for the pallets. This was nothing Shawn hadn't done up until a year ago. Ron followed Tanner toward the pallets as Shawn headed for the lift outside.

Shawn leaped up onto the lift, not thinking anything of it until he felt dizzy. He sat down in the driver's seat and paused for a moment. That's all it took to get his mind worried about the feelings he was having and throw him right into a full-blown panic attack. He tried to fight it and just start the engine to the lift, but the attack overtook him and he turned it off.

"Don't give in to panic," he told himself and started the engine once more. He was forgetting to do his breathing and relaxation techniques and his physical feelings were winning over his thoughts. His body felt hot, his hands started shaking and his pulse raced.

"What's that about?" Tanner heard the motor of the lift go on and off again. He didn't know if something was wrong with the lift or with Shawn, but he knew something wasn't right.

Tanner headed out of the shed to check on his brother as Ron followed behind thinking the lift must be broken. Shawn was trying to get off the lift but was too unstable. Tanner hurried over to help him down.

"Shawn, are you okay?" Tanner steadied his arms and turned him around to see his face.

"No, I need to get to the house." His voice shook as he tried to pull away from Tanner to run for the house. He was terrified and embarrassed.

"Oh, come on Shawn! Suck it up," Ron said, frustrated. "You're okay, just get back to work and you'll be fine." He thought his tough tone and comments might actually help Shawn get control again, since none of the women were around to coddle him. He figured that if he embarrassed

Shawn, he would get back up on the lift, finish his job, and the panic attack would stop.

He was clearly wrong.

Shawn went pale and sweat droplets rapidly began to appear all over his face as his whole body began to tremble.

"Shut up, Ron, and go get Rachel," Tanner demanded as he gave Ron an angry look and hung on to Shawn, making sure he didn't let him run. Ron took a closer look at Shawn as his symptoms worsened rapidly. He looked bad. Ron quickly realized that this wasn't just a little panic attack, just as Rebecca had warned, and now he felt bad. *This guy has a serious problem,* Ron realized. As fast as possible, he took off for the main house to get Rachel.

"Shawn, you're going to be fine, just relax and do your breathing," Tanner tried to encourage him, even though Tanner was a wreck inside, worried for his brother. Shawn was very pale, shaking very hard and his whole body was beginning to sweat now, not just his face. If Tanner didn't know better, he'd think Shawn had some horrible illness.

"I'm not fine, I need to go into the house." Shawn tried again to head for the house, jerking one arm away from Tanner.

"Just sit down and rest here for just a minute, then I'll let you go back to the house," Tanner grabbed hold of him again, forcing Shawn to stay. Rachel had told him not to let Shawn run back to the house and Tanner was trying everything he could think of to keep him from doing that, but time was running out. He could only keep Shawn still for so long. "Do the breathing Rachel showed you," Tanner tried to remind him.

Shawn tried to relax his arms and do his breathing like Rachel had taught him. He wanted the panic attack to stop but his breathing was hindered, and his arms tightened right back up.

"It's not working, I need to get to the house." He was breathing fast and hard, barely catching his breath. He looked like he was going to pass out at any minute.

Ron threw open the front door of the main house, banging it into the wall and startling the women in the kitchen. As they looked in the direction of the noise, Ron frantically entered the room.

"Hurry, it's Shawn, he's having a bad attack." Ron turned to Rachel, out of breath from running, "Tanner said to get you."

Rachel hurried out of the house right behind Ron. Rachel knew it had to be a bad one for Ron to be upset. Victoria and Rebecca tried to follow.

"No, don't follow. Wait here or it will make things worse for Shawn," Rachel told them, putting her hand out in the air to stop them as she continued to follow Ron. She knew from her own experience, the more people around, the more tense the situation would become.

When Rachel and Ron got to Shawn, he stared up at Rachel and she saw the terror in his eyes. He was having a bad attack all right and his eyes were desperate for her help. Tanner looked desperate as well, hoping that Rachel would know what to do.

"It's okay, I've got him Tanner, go back to work," she pointed at the building where Tanner had been working as she knelt down next to Shawn. She knew Shawn needed to hear that he would be all right and for no one to be watching him. Embarrassment was not what he needed.

"Are you sure?" Tanner questioned, concerned at leaving her with this situation alone, knowing Shawn might just take off on her or collapse.

"Yes, Shawn will be fine, just give him a minute," she gave Tanner a look that said they needed to be alone.

"Okay, Ron, let's get back to work." Tanner directed Ron back towards the building, wanting to do whatever was best for the situation. They went back inside the building, leaving Shawn and Rachel alone.

"Shawn, you're going to be okay," Rachel looked him in the eyes.

"No, I'm not, I need to go in the house," he argued, short of breath and turning his face away.

"No, you need to practice what you've learned."

"It's not working," he claimed, looking towards the ground, ashamed and sounding like he was about to cry. He felt out of control and beaten.

"How many times have you told yourself that in the last five minutes? It's not working because you're convincing yourself it won't work," she tried to reason.

"No, really, I tried and it didn't work." He really felt it wasn't working this time.

"Prove it to me," she debated sternly.

"What do you mean 'prove it?'" He looked at her now, confused, and he couldn't believe she was challenging him when he was sick like this.

"Do your breathing and relaxation and then let's see if it doesn't work," she challenged.

"Okay," he agreed, slightly angry, and began trying to slow down his breathing.

"That's good, you're breathing slower, but you're not stomach breathing. It's important you do the stomach breathing. Breathe out then hold it to the count of five before you breathe in again," her voice was gentle now.

He focused on his breathing, doing just as she said. "Breathe long slow breaths. Not short fast ones." She showed him as she did it herself. Once he did it a few times correctly she moved on to his muscle relaxation.

"Notice how tight your shoulders are? You're totally tense. Let your shoulders fall. Feel them drop. Now, relax your arm and hand muscles," she rubbed his arms and hands briefly, helping him to relax and making sure he was letting the muscles go limp. "Close your eyes now and just focus on your breathing and relaxation, nothing else."

He did as she said and quickly the sweating and shaking was gone. He was breathing normally again. He opened his eyes and gave her a slight smile, fearing that if he became confident it would come back. After a couple of minutes, he had to admit, "It worked. I feel a lot better."

"I'm sorry you had to go through this Shawn, but I want you to realize it does work. You stopped the attack by doing all the relaxation techniques and by not giving up."

"You're right," he agreed. "At first, it wasn't working but when I kept trying, it suddenly kicked in and the attack just stopped," he said, amazed.

"Don't fear panic attacks, just expect them to come, because they will. But if you expect them, you'll be prepared instead of scared."

"I know. It came out of nowhere. I just got on the lift, felt dizzy, then boom, it hit me." He sat up, more relaxed now, as he described what happened.

"Maybe it hit because when you felt dizzy, you got afraid of the feeling. You were afraid a panic attack was coming so you brought one on. Next time you feel dizzy, just start your slow stomach breathing, relax your muscles, and ride the wave. Remind yourself to let the panic come, don't fight it. Float through it and it will disappear. Once you practice it enough, you'll be able to do it while you're working or even watching a movie. You'll eventually be able to do it without anyone aware that you're doing it." Rachel explained it like a wonderful secret, and it was, to him. He had a cure for what he felt was a horrible disease.

They stood up and Rachel insisted he shouldn't hurry back to the house.

"You need to stay out here for a little bit to make sure you know that being outside didn't bring on the attack. It can happen anywhere. I don't want you feeling your bedroom is your only safe spot."

Shawn's emotions were like a roller coaster. One minute he felt as if he has a way of beating these phobias, the next he is discouraged and feeling like an outcast.

"Why can't I just be like my brother? He's like a Real Hero. He saves everyone and fears nothing. You should have seen him when my dad's arm was stuck. I couldn't believe what he did to get him free. He just took charge without hesitation and did what needed to be done to save him. Why can't I be like that?"

"You are like that. You were right there helping in an emergency, putting all your own fears aside. Another thing, Tanner gets afraid just like everyone else does at one time or another. You better believe he was afraid when he was trying to save your dad and when he was fighting that alligator to save the pilot. He even told you he was. The difference is that he doesn't think about his fears and feelings at the time. He focuses on the other people in need and does whatever needs to be done to help them. You can be just like that, you've already proved that by being in there when your dad needed help. All you have to do now is work on not fearing your panic attacks and practice your relaxation techniques then you'll be a Real Hero before you know it," she encouraged, giving him a smile and nod of confidence.

Tanner and Ron had been watching from inside the building. They came out, moved by Shawn's efforts and determination not to run home but to stay and wait out his panic attack. His color was back and his sweats were gone.

"Hey buddy, feeling better?" Tanner asked, giving Shawn's arm a gentle nudge.

"Yeah, much. I'm sorry about all this," Shawn said, embarrassed.

"No Shawn, I'm sorry," Ron came forward, "I didn't realize it was this bad for you. I used to have panic attacks when I was young but nothing like this and I made it worse for you. I'm really sorry, man." He gave Shawn a pat on the arm, trying to assure him he'd be supportive from now on.

"That's okay, Ron." Shawn was glad Ron didn't think he was a wimp anymore and understood more of what he had been dealing with. It gave Shawn encouragement to try even harder, knowing he had the support instead of feeling like a useless coward.

"It was actually a good thing this happened," Rachel said to the men, with a smile. They all looked at her like she was crazy. "No, I'm serious. He needed the practice for the harvest."

None of the men could believe she was bringing up helping with the harvest right now after what Shawn had just been through. However, she knew the harvest picking was the most important event of the year for their whole family and he missed it last year. She didn't want him to miss it this year.

"But I couldn't even do this lift without an attack, how do you feel I can be ready for the harvest? Obviously, I'm not ready," he questioned her. He looked at her with confusion, as if she might know something he didn't. He wanted badly to be included at the harvest, did she have a plan? It seemed she usually did when it came to his panic attacks.

"If you don't think you're ready then you better get up there and finish what you started," she pointed at the lift. All the men looked at her with disbelief. "Remember what we just talked about: building your confidence. I'll be right here if you have another attack and you can practice your breathing and relaxation again if it happens. I don't think you'll have another attack right now because if you start to feel dizzy you know what to do, right? Just ride it out like a wave and let it pass," she reminded him. She looked into his eyes, giving him a look that encouraged him to make this his first step towards being like his brother and working past his fear.

"Right," he agreed, then looked at Tanner and Ron for their reaction. They looked at him like the ball was in his court now. Only he would know whether he was ready to push himself or not. He chose to get up on the lift again without hesitation while Tanner and Ron gave him a proud nod, then headed for the pallets.

As the men worked, lifting and moving pallets, Rachel could see Victoria and Rebecca from a distance, they were outside watching. They could see that everything was okay now or the men wouldn't be working again. Rachel was glad for Victoria. Between her husband and son, she's been through a lot lately and could use a break. Watching her son collect himself, learning to control his phobias, and continue to work was a big positive. Even from that distance, Rachel could see the joy in her face.

***

That night before dinner, Tanner and Ron told the women to go get dressed up because they had a surprise for them. They got dressed up as well. Tanner loaned Ron a jacket and tie. Ron still hadn't caved in to buy his own yet, but Tanner felt sure it wouldn't be long before he did, dating Rebecca. She got him to do things they never thought he would do.

Ron was still feeling low about when he and Rebecca went out recently. Ron noticed Rebecca glancing towards a handsome man dressed up in a suit jacket and tie. There was no way Ron wasn't going to show her that he was capable of doing the same. When Rebecca saw him, her face beamed. She knew he must care a great deal about her to go to this extent to impress her.

"You look really handsome," she whispered as she wrapped her arm around his and gave him a flirtatious smile.

"Thank you beautiful, glad you approve," he said, feeling very successful in his efforts.

Tanner was used to dressing up for important functions with his job so this came easy for him. Rachel thought he looked as handsome and sophisticated as always, fitting his role as the winery owner.

Rachel and Rebecca had borrowed a couple of Victoria's evening gowns to really impress the men, which they did.

The women didn't know where they were going but they were excited to be going out and having fun. Even if they only ended up at the winery restaurant, that would be fine with them. It had romantic, dark lighting and live music for dancing.

Neil and Victoria sent them off, telling them to have a good time.

"Have fun at the prom, kids," Shawn whispered to himself with a chuckle. He enjoyed watching the close friendship they had together.

They all got into Tanner's new car, which told the girls it wasn't the winery restaurant they were going to or they'd just walk.

However, they were wrong. Tanner drove the car to the back entrance of the restaurant and parked, surprising them. He just wanted to throw them off by driving the car.

"What is going on?" Rachel asked Tanner as he politely helped her out of the car, ever the gentleman. She was curious as to why they weren't going in the front door.

"You'll see," he gave her an amused smile, reading the question on her face.

Rebecca had an idea of what was going on. *If we're going in the back door we might get to walk through the kitchen and see it.* She had high hopes. "Are we going to walk through the kitchen?" she asked Ron, all charged up.

"You'll see." Ron gave the same response as Tanner, not wanting to ruin the surprise.

As she had hoped, Tanner led them through the back door and right into the kitchen.

Chapter 13

The kitchen was filled with staff in white coats and white chef hats. The room was permeated with mouth-watering smells of barbecued meats and seasonings. The head chef was obvious by his double-breasted white jacket with black buttons and black piping on the collar and cuffs. The black piping traveled all the way down the center front of his jacket.

Upon seeing Tanner, the head chef came right over to greet him and meet his guests. He had known Tanner and his family for many years and couldn't wait to meet Tanner's new bride.

Tanner introduced Rachel proudly, then Rebecca and Ron. The chef was all smiles as he gave Rachel's hand a quick kiss, making her blush.

"Don't let us interrupt your work Antoine, I know how busy you are on a Saturday night," Tanner assured him as a waiter appeared to direct Tanner and his guest to their seating.

It was an extremely busy night for the restaurant but with the harvest due to start any night now and Rebecca due back to the college soon, Tanner didn't have any other day available.

Rachel and Rebecca gave each other a delighted look then gawked at the whole kitchen not wanting to miss a single thing as they slowly followed the waiter. They saw different types of stainless-steel stoves and ovens as well as long counters for prep work.

There were ladles hanging from the ceiling, down just low enough for the cooks to reach but not so low they were in the way while preparing food. There were two levels of shelves below the long prep counters. One was layered neatly with different pots and pans. The second was layered with different sizes of plates and bowls. Everything was within arm's reach for quick preparations and service.

Rachel noticed the huge six-burner gas range with cast iron burners. Huge pots were filled with something delicious inside. Rebecca guessed it to be pasta. Rachel guessed it to be lobster or crab.

One huge barbeque grill had six good size steaks and three racks of lamb cooking on it at the same time. Rachel wondered how they knew when each cut of meat would be done to the right temperature when cooking so many at once.

Rebecca noticed a large rotisserie oven to her right with eight whole chickens turning as they cooked, dripping mouth-watering juices. To her left were two large fish laying on thick ice, waiting to be cooked when it was time.

All of the cooks seemed very organized in their own stations for their own food preparation duties.

The waiter directed Tanner and his guests over to a table for four that had been brought in and set up in the kitchen just for their use. It was complete with table settings, wine glasses, and lit candles.

"Now you both can watch the chef, his sous chef, and the rest of the cooks as they make magic here in the kitchen for you and the other guests," Tanner announced proudly as he held a chair out for Rachel to sit and Ron held a chair for Rebecca. As they sat down, the waiter placed a napkin on each one of their laps.

"This is unbelievable!" Rebecca whispered to Rachel with a big smile.

"Tanner, this is wonderful. I can't believe you set this up for us," Rachel touched his arm gently but couldn't take her eyes off what was going on in the kitchen. She and Rebecca had spent many late nights falling asleep to cooking shows and now they were seeing one in person.

"Ron and I both planned it out," Tanner shared the glory, giving a nod in Ron's direction.

Rebecca squeezed Ron's hand and gave him a warm smile of appreciation.

"What may I get you to drink?" The gentleman waiter looked at Rachel first. But the furthest thing on Rachel's mind right now was what drink she wanted. Her mind was on this magical moment, getting to be in the kitchen watching real chefs at work.

"Just give us each a glass of our usual reserve, please Scott," Tanner told him, knowing it was the top of the line and everyone would like it. Scott smiled, enjoying the women's excitement. He was obviously familiar with the preferred wines of the Reed family.

Rebecca watched as a salamander broiler was being used to melt cheese over certain dishes. She remembered from the cooking shows how the salamander broiler would melt cheeses and caramelize and grill foods without the fear of burning them.

Rachel watched as workers put together fancy pizzas, then placed them in a very large, round, wood fire pizza oven. She was enjoying the large range of foods prepared at this restaurant. No wonder they needed so many cooks.

Rebecca could see a special refrigerator used to store fresh vegetables of all sorts. Peppers were in their own covered containers as well as onion, carrots, broccoli, and cauliflower. All were sealed, labeled and organized.

Rachel noticed the large walk-in refrigerator that workers went in to get their fresh meats, poultry and fish. She couldn't help but wonder how cold the workers were each time they went in there.

"Look at their range of prep foods over there," Rachel told Rebecca, pointing at the area where the prep cooks were in a line making salads. In front of them were containers of chopped onions, carrots, cucumbers, corn, beets, broccoli, different colored peppers, mushrooms, jalapeno peppers, shredded cheeses and more. It was clear those prep cooks had to have washed, cut and prepared all those ingredients before the restaurant opened for the dinner rush.

Rebecca smiled as she looked over the prep foods Rachel had mentioned, then she pointed out a wedge cutter that was cutting potatoes into any size and shape that was needed in just seconds.

"Amazing! And look at that!" Rachel gestured in the direction of a huge tray of corn on the cob, shucked on skewers, already stabbed through and waiting to go on the grill when needed.

They were excited like two little kids at Disneyland. Watching all the cooks preparing food in such a large quantity, quickly and professionally, was such a treat.

"Rachel, you're going to need to order your dinner, then you can keep staring some more," Tanner teased with an amused look.

"Rebecca, that would be a good idea for you too before the restaurant closes." Ron joined in on the playful harassment.

"Oh, stop." Rebecca hit Ron's arm, joking back at him. "Give me that menu." She took the menu out of his hand.

Rebecca wasn't the only person acting silly. Later that night, Ron did his share when the food started to arrive. Once they put his steak in front of him, he was asking for salt.

"Shhhh," Rebecca quickly whispered to him.

"Why are you shhhshing me?" he asked. Rachel joined in, whispering for him not to speak so loudly.

"What?" He was really lost but lowered his voice to a whisper just the same. "I just asked for salt?"

"You never ask for salt or ketchup at a fancy restaurant like this, it's an insult to the chef. His food should be able to stand on its own without salt or ketchup once it is served. I'm sure if you taste it you'll agree," Rebecca warned with a whisper.

Ron looked at Rebecca then Tanner with a serious look that said, *These women have lost their minds.*

Tanner knew that it would be an insult to the chef if he did ask for salt, but he didn't want Ron to feel uncomfortable either. He shrugged his shoulders trying to make light of the situation and suggested, "Give it a taste and see if you still feel it needs it afterwards."

Ron kept calm and tasted the steak, trying to be a good sport and go along with Tanner. Everyone waited and watched, trying to anticipate his reaction. A pause was followed by a slow, broad smile of pleasure.

Tanner had known that a single bite might take care of the problem and it did. The chef had used top grade meat, dry brined in kosher salt and pepper for 24 hours. The French technique effectively permeated the cut of meat and tenderized it at the same time. The combination made the steak savory in flavor and irresistible.

As they ate their meal, the women continued to watch carefully as the cooks prepared dishes, enjoying every minute of the live show. Afterwards, the head chef came over to visit with Tanner and his guests. The dinner rush was slowing down and he wanted to see if they enjoyed their meals. They assured the chef that the meals were exceptional and told him how much they appreciated his letting them be in there watching as he prepared it.

"Thank you, Antoine, I really appreciate this," Tanner shook his hand.

"Do you have any questions I can answer for you?" Antoine turned his attention to the women. He was a very professional and friendly man in his early 50's with a strong French accent to match his name.

"One question each," Ron jumped in abruptly, knowing the women could get carried away. "He doesn't have all night." Ron was starting to get a little bored with it all himself. This wasn't his thing, that was for sure. He was tolerating it for Rebecca's sake, and she knew it, which meant a lot to her but she still gave Ron a scrunched brow as a warning to continue being patient or else. She asked her question to the chef. "When I watch these cooking shows on TV, chefs are always tasting the food as they cook. Why aren't they worried about spreading germs in all the food?"

Rachel cringed at the question, slightly embarrassed, even though it was a fair question. She was just surprised that Rebecca had asked it of the chef who had just prepared her food, probably tasting it as he went.

Ron couldn't help but give out with a smirk and Rebecca kicked him under the table.

"That's a good question," the chef replied. He walked over to the cooking area and pointed to a container that was full of mini spoons. He lifted one of the spoons, tasted the gravy in the pan closest to him, then pointed at another small container where he placed the dirty spoon.

"Oh my, I didn't even see those." Rebecca thought that the system was very ingenious. "Well I'm relieved."

Everyone started laughing.

"What about you Rachel?" Tanner encouraged. He knew she'd be just as excited to ask a question.

"I'd like to know what the name Sous Chef means. It sounds like it's a French word, maybe?" It wasn't a big question, but one she's wondered about forever and never took the time to research.

"You're correct, it is French. It means 'under-chef of the kitchen' which means he is second in command in the kitchen," the chef explained.

"That makes sense," she was pleased with his answer and proud that she was right about the origin of the name.

Ron was right about only having time for one question each because the chef got called away right after answering Rachel's question. The women looked fascinated and gratified from the whole experience. Tanner and Ron felt proud, they had done something very special for their women that night.

"What do you say we top this evening off over there on the dance floor?" Tanner stood up, putting his hand out to his wife. He knew she'd love the slow, live music that was being played in the main restaurant.

"I would love to," she took his hand, giving him a warm smile as she stood up.

"Ready for me to show you how it's done?" Ron asked Rebecca as he stood up, putting his hand out to her. He knew she would be anxious to dance and try to show him up as usual.

"Right, you show me, or at least you'll try to," she bantered, taking his hand and standing.

It was a perfect, relaxing evening, exactly what both couples needed before the actual harvesting work would begin. They knew it could be any day but what they didn't know was Neil would be announcing it tomorrow night.

***

The next night, Neil made the announcement right after dinner.

"Sleep well tonight everyone because tomorrow night we will be out in the vines." Neil declared with a big smile on his face as he lifted his glass of wine 'to the beginning of the harvest.'

"Yahoo!" Tanner, Ron and Shawn all yelled, pleased with the good news. It was finally time. This was a big thing for wine growers. Rachel and Rebecca beamed at the thought of their first harvest and the big event.

"Have you told Juan and all the other workers?" Tanner asked his dad.

"Yes, just before I came in and they're all overjoyed," he replied, pulling his wife near to him to enjoy his excitement.

"Weather is supposed to be perfect and we'll get out there at 2:00 a.m. to make sure we have plenty of time before the heat comes," Neil continued.

"Can I call Dave to help with the harvesting? He's helped before." Shawn was beside himself with excitement.

"Sure Shawn, the more hands the better." His father was thrilled to have Shawn wanting his friend around again. Shawn left the table in a hurry, anxious to call his friend.

"Hey, what about dinner?" his dad questioned.

"I'll be right back, Dad," Shawn's voice echoed as he hurried out of the kitchen.

Everyone was pleased to see Shawn so eager. Everyone except Tanner. He was a little concerned as he glanced at Rachel, wondering if she thought it was too soon for Shawn to be diving into working in the vineyard. He had the recent experience of having been with Shawn when everything went south with him.

"It'll be okay, just keep me and Shawn working in the same area," she assured Tanner.

"Okay beautiful, you know best," Tanner felt relieved.

"The girls and I will get to the grocery store first thing after breakfast to get the food," Victoria assured her husband. She knew what her job was for the harvest: food preparations. Having everyone working hard would require plenty of food and drinks to be brought to them throughout the days while picking continued.

"What are we making?" Rachel asked, she could see Rebecca was just as curious.

"There are going to be a lot of hungry and thirsty pickers as they harvest the grapes but none of them will want to stop picking to eat. You see, the faster they pick the sooner they're done and the sooner they get paid. Everyone has waited for this all year. Some of them have bills that have built up during the year and the big bonus they get when we're done will help them pay their debts.

That means we need to make small, easy to eat meals that they can grab and keep working. Things like breakfast biscuits with sausage, burritos, tacos, cookies and more. We'll also load up on lots of bottles of water," Victoria explained in detail.

"What happens when they need to use the bathroom after all that water?" Rebecca asked with a half chuckle. Rachel snickered, not surprised at the classic Rebecca-type questioning.

"Everyone has to bring their own plastic bag with them just in case they have to go," Ron told her with a serious tone.

"What!" Rebecca screeched, disgusted. She turned to look at Ron hoping it was a joke, but she wasn't laughing.

"He's teasing you," Tanner quickly intervened with a chuckle. "We already have portable toilets scattered throughout the vineyard for the crew to use. Our fields are far too big for the pickers to come all the way back to the winery every time they need to use the restroom and we certainly don't want them doing it by the grapes. The port-a-potties have washing stations at them as well to make sure everyone washes their hands before going back to picking."

"That's a relief," Rebecca said, finally releasing the breath she had been holding. She looked at Rachel, knowing she must have been disgusted by the thought. "Nice one, Ron," Rebecca gave Ron a revengeful look. He got her good on that one but payback was coming.

Shawn came hustling back through the kitchen door. "Dave will be here first thing in the morning to help get things ready then he'll just stay here as long as we need him. He can stay in my room with me."

"Sounds good!" His dad was overjoyed to see his son this happy again. "He'll be paid like everyone else for all the days he works."

"All the days he's here? What do you mean?" Rachel asked, confused. She had figured the harvest was just the one night.

"To harvest the different types of grapes for the different red wines, it will take a good week or two to get done. It doesn't happen in just one night. Some are picked earlier than others depending on the taste we're after," Tanner explained. "Depending on the sun exposure and soil, which is different in some areas of the vineyard, some of the grapes won't be ready to be picked until even later than that."

"Oh my," she was shocked. "That's a long time. You get up in the middle of the night, every night to do this?"

"We hire extra workers to come in, making it where we can switch off and get some rest. Without a doubt everyone still ends up exhausted. But if you or Rebecca get tired, don't be afraid to stop because we have plenty of workers that are used to this hard work. I don't want you two overdoing it." Tanner knew it would be hard on them, being their first time. It was a hard schedule and continuous work.

"I can't miss school for that long, but I'll stay as long as I can." Rebecca wasn't afraid of hard work. She loved the challenge.

"I'll be okay. I can do it. I want to be with you," Rachel told Tanner, but the look on her face wasn't very convincing. She wanted to be by his side but whether she'd be able to last two weeks, or even longer maybe, she didn't know. She hadn't been feeling her best the last few days.

Later that night, when everyone else went to bed, Tanner talked to Rachel.

"Are you okay hon? You're not yourself today." He pulled her close once they got into bed.

"Yes, I think I just need to get outside and do something rather than stay inside as much as I do. I'm sure I'll feel better out there picking grapes in the fresh air with my husband," she smiled, then gave him a kiss.

"I know I'll like it a lot more having you next to me," Tanner gave her a comforting smile.

As Rachel dozed off in the warmth and safety of Tanner's arms, she was concerned for herself more than she wanted to let on. *I hope that's all it is because I really don't feel well lately.*

***

The next morning, the women made breakfast for the men, then Victoria and Rebecca hurried off to get food fixings. The men had plenty of work to do themselves to get things ready for the harvest that night. Rachel waited at the house and worked on more food preparations. She didn't want to be far from where Shawn was outside working.

After the two women returned, they all spent the rest of the morning making lots of food and wrapping each item individually. This would now make it easy for everyone to just grab some food as they headed out and to deliver food later to the crew. Everything would be packed in special containers to keep the food warm and the drinks cold. Rachel could tell they have been doing this routine for many years and she was thrilled to be a part of it now.

There was much to do in such a short amount of time to have the meals prepared for all the workers for the next day. The women hardly had time to make lunch for themselves and their own men. They quickly threw some sandwiches together, added chips, and collapsed in their chairs while joining their men for lunch.

"Tired already?" Ron teased Rebecca.

"Don't worry, I'll work you into the ground during the picking," she challenged him, sitting up straighter as if to show him she could handle it.

While Ron and Rebecca did their usual bantering, Tanner stood up, taking half his sandwich, and went to the counter to make Rachel a plate of food. He added her favorite fruit and chips.

"I made you a plate of your favorites," he told her as he placed the plate in front of her. He was worried about her. She had been working hard preparing the meals but he hadn't seen her eat anything the whole morning.

"No, I don't think so," she replied, looking at it with a nauseous expression on her face. "After making so much food, I don't have much of an appetite. Thank you, though.

Maybe later," she gave him a slight grin. She did appreciate how he watched over her all the time.

"I'll eat hers." Shawn reached over her shoulder, grabbing the plate. His appetite was coming back. He didn't realize Rachel felt bad or he wouldn't have teased her about her food.

Dave laughed at him as Shawn took the plate and sat back in the seat next to him. Rachel could tell Dave was very happy to have his friend back to normal.

"It's about time you had an appetite again. You've been eating like a bird," Neil commented. His tone was teasing but the statement was true.

"Well, I feel great," he told his dad, and he did. He had worked outside with the other men and his friend the whole morning, feeling totally himself again. He had no signs of any panic attacks and he felt great, like his life was given back to him.

"That's so good to hear, honey," Victoria beamed at her son's joy and success.

When the women finished cleaning up the kitchen, Rachel and Rebecca decided to go outside to see what their men and all the workers were doing at the last minute before the big event that night.

Chapter 14

The winery grounds were like a highway of workers with people and machines going every which way. They all seem to know their destinations, though. Some were preparing tall light fixtures for the night picking. Some were driving pallets full of bins to put the grapes in once they were picked.

Rachel and Rebecca saw Shawn and Dave drive by on a tractor hauling some of the big bins as well. They waved to them as they went by and Shawn looked like a new person, all smiles and talking away to his friend.

"He's doing very well." Rebecca smiled as she watched them drive off.

"Yeah, I'm happy for him. I hope this harvest picking goes well for him; it means so much to him." Rachel hurried across the dirt road to get out of the way of a work truck that was en route to its destination.

"I wonder where we'll be working tonight?" Rebecca looked around at the various fields full of grapes.

"We'll be at the top of the hill over there," Rachel turned to the left and pointed way off in the distance to a very high hill.

Rebecca's eyes opened wide. "Wow! That looks like a true challenge."

"That big harvest tractor can't work on that hill safely and Tanner told me that some of their best grapes are up there," Rachel explained.

Rebecca chuckled. "Big harvest tractor thing?" she teased. "It's a Mechanical Grape Harvester. You're going to have to learn the names of most of this stuff now that you married someone who owns a winery."

"I know, it's like going to college for wine making just living here. By the way, how did you know what it's called?" Rachel asked as she spotted Tanner out the corner of her eye. Tanner, Neil and Ron were all standing together discussing the plans. Tanner raised his arm and pointed toward the hill Rachel had mentioned.

"You told me when I first got here silly," Rebecca chattered on, not paying attention to the men. "You already forgot the name of it, just like in college," she teased with a slight laugh.

Rachel could overhear Tanner assuring his dad, "We'll get that done and out of the way first thing, then everything else will seem easy." Tanner smiled the minute he spotted Rachel. "Hey beautiful, what are you women up to?" He hurried over, reaching out and pulling her gently next to him. Still the newlyweds, he just needed to feel their closeness and she was pleased he did.

"We are just checking things out and planning for tonight," Rachel replied.

"Hey, tough guy," Rebecca went over to Ron, giving him a gentle slug on the arm.

"Come here, woman," he teased. He put his arm around her waist as he tried to keep his dirty gloves off of her clothes, then pulled her close, delivering an overly dramatic kiss on her lips.

Tanner, Rachel, and Neil laughed, enjoying the couple's playful side.

Tanner continued his conversation with his dad, still holding on to Rachel. Neil questioned Tanner first, "That's going to get the workers tired right off by doing the hardest area first, don't you think?"

"Yes, but I'll only take the six of us and a few of our strongest workers who can handle it up there. The rest will be in the lower fields," Tanner explained. "I want to make sure those grapes get picked before anything can happen to them, they're some of our best grapes."

"Okay son, then that's the plan." He gave his son a proud pat on the back and a friendly smile to everyone else before he left.

"Now for the more important things," Tanner turned to face Rachel and gave her a warm kiss.

"How's it going?" she asked, after the nice greeting.

"As much as I want you with me, I still think you should be in the other fields on flat land, not on that hillside tonight," Tanner warned as he stared into her beautiful green eyes.

"I want to be by my husband's side, working," she pleaded as she peered into his dark brown eyes. The passion in their eyes spoke volumes, they didn't need words. It was obvious to all that a warm current of love shot though both of them any time they were together.

Tanner didn't have much time to talk though, he had to get everything ready for tonight. He did take the time to warn the women about what clothes to wear. "You need to have mom show you where the work clothes are kept. You'll need some thick denim jeans, a long sleeve shirt and we have some nice big hats you'll both love," he said with an evil grin, knowing the women aren't going to love their attire by any means.

"Oh, this is going to be good," Ron said with a chuckle, knowing this was going to drive the women crazy.

"Oh hush!" Rebecca jabbed his side with her elbow.

"What?" Rachel objected in a sharp tone, hoping he was joking.

"I'm sorry but I am serious. You're going to be working with lots of thorns and even bees. It's extremely sticky work and it will stain any clothes you wear."

"Why the clown hat? Why can't we just wear our caps?" Rebecca questioned.

"When it comes up, that sun is brutal out there in the fields, but you can wear your caps if it will make you feel better," he surrendered. "You'll probably need a sweatshirt over your shirt early in the morning," he continued, "but remember, anything you wear will end up stained."

"Okay then, let's go plan out our wardrobe, Rachel." Rebecca waved her hand for Rachel to follow as she left Ron and headed for the house.

"Okay, I guess I'll see you later." She gave Tanner another quick peck on the lips and off they went.

"Hey Rachel," Tanner called out to her as she was walking away.

Rachel and Rebecca stopped and turned in his direction.

"Shawn seems to be doing great out there," he said, pleased, hoping she felt the same way.

"Yes, he is," she replied in agreement, making his day. He didn't want any distractions tonight. Everyone needed to be on their 'A' game.

As they were walking back to the house, Rebecca mentioned that their clothes would probably be drenched with grape juice by the time they were done.

"Actually, the whole object is to not break the skins of the grapes. You see, we're hand-harvesting them so the skins won't break open and we're doing it early in the morning that way the grapes won't get warm, otherwise they'd prematurely ferment and that's not good," Rachel explained.

"Well now, I'm impressed. I guess you have been learning a little about this wine making stuff from your husband." Rebecca bumped her hip against Rachel, teasing her, and Rachel bumped back. "Will we be sorting the grapes later after they're done picking them?" Rebecca wondered.

"I don't think we will. They have conveyor belts and machines that do all of the sorting. They only need a few people by the conveyor belts to make sure nothing wrong gets past, and someone else to keep the machines running. I doubt they'll need us."

"How does the machines know the difference between good grapes and bad grapes? Or a twig or leaf?" Rebecca was very curious.

"They have a laser that sees everything and can tell if the grape is the right size, shape and even color. If it's not right, the machine blows it over to a different conveyor belt to separate it away from the good grapes."

"That's awesome. I hope we get to be there at some point just to see it work. It sounds interesting to watch." Rebecca wanted to be part of everything, but time was running out before she had to be back at her college.

"Me too. I'm sure Tanner will arrange for us to watch the machine work if I ask him," Rachel assured her.

Bedtime came early for everyone, but it was hard for Rachel to get any rest, she was too keyed up. Apparently, Shawn and Dave were as well because she could hear them joking and laughing in Shawn's room.

No one took the time to eat dinner. It was more important for them to get what little rest they could before the picking started. They would get a snack going out the door and burritos or tacos delivered to them later, while they were picking the grapes. That was okay with Rachel because she didn't have an appetite anyway.

The more she thought about it, the more Rachel started getting worried about the picking. She was concerned that she might slow Tanner down, being a beginner. She knew that if she couldn't keep up, he would slow down to stay with her and that would make him get behind. Timing was very important with the harvest and she didn't want to mess that up. *I'm just going to have to go as fast as I can and keep up.* She was determined not to let him down.

At 2:30 a.m. a loud horn in the winery blew, waking everyone up. It was a horn that was also used if there was an emergency in the vineyard from fire or frost; a way for the whole winery to be awakened quickly to save the grapes.

After quickly dressing, Rachel and Rebecca met in the hallway. They took one look at each other's attire and started laughing. They were both wearing thick blue denim jeans and flannel checkered shirts.

"I feel like a farmer," Rebecca looked down at her clothes.

"I feel like I'm going to pick cotton," Rachel held up her arms, looking at her flannel shirt sleeves.

"Keep walking ladies," Tanner encouraged from behind, taking Rachel's shoulders and steering her towards the stairs. Time was wasting, in his eyes, and he didn't want them to take time to rethink their attire.

Victoria was stationed at the bottom of the steps as everyone hurried down the stairs to get out the front door and into the vineyard. She had a tray of coffee and donuts to hand each person as they shot past.

Rachel and Rebecca gave each other a warm smile as they watched the routine everyone had for this event.

"Thank you, this is so sweet." Rachel took a coffee but not a donut.

"I know Rachel well enough already to know she can't function without her coffee in the morning," Victoria said with a smile.

"And I can't live without the donuts," Rebecca replied with a smile as she took two.

"Thanks, Mom," Tanner gave his mom a kiss on the cheek as he hurried pass.

Ron and the boys thanked her also as they filed out the front door. Neil was nowhere in sight, but Rachel figured he was probably the one who blew the loud horn.

Ron, Rebecca, Shawn, Dave, two men and a woman all climbed into the back of a truck. Tanner got behind the wheel and Rachel sat up front with him. He drove them to the top of the hillside where they would be picking the grapes. Rachel was grateful for the ride because she would have been exhausted before they even got started if she had to walk up that steep hillside.

"We'll start at the top and work a few rows at a time coming down the hill. That will be the easiest way," Tanner explained. "Once we get to the bottom of the hill, Tony is going to have the truck down there to give us all a ride back up to the top." The field was big with many rows of grapes and would take many trips.

Tanner stopped the truck and the people and the supplies were quickly unloaded. Tony got out of the back and climbed into the driver's seat to head back down the hill. He was a muscular man, full of energy. He had probably been taking care of the vines on this hill for many years.

Tanner had everyone grab what looked to Rachel like a pair of sharp garden shears and a bin to carry the grapes. He showed them how to hold and cut the grape bundles quickly but gently. He explained the difference in size, color and feel for the good versus bad grapes. He only wanted them to pick the best grapes and leave everything else for the workers. They would come back after the best grapes were picked to get rid of anything bad and to shape the vines. Tanner explained everything very quickly but thoroughly and the picking began.

"Don't try to lift your bin, just slide it along as you work your way down the hill. There will be quads pulling flatbeds following behind us. We will put our full bins on there and they will give us empty ones as we go," Tanner explained.

Rachel noticed there were two different quads that followed close behind the pickers, as Tanner had mentioned. There was a rotation they followed: driving up the hillside to pick up the full bins, then taking them down to the bottom where other workers waited to empty them into a huge container, then driving back up again for more full bins. At the bottom, a tractor would pick up the huge container once it was filled with grapes and take it to the winery to be sorted and eventually crushed.

She also noted how the drivers could only put a certain amount of bins on the back of the flatbeds that the quads were pulling, otherwise the weight would push them all the way down the hill. The routine they had worked beautifully, Rachel was very impressed.

A couple of hours went by and everyone stopped their work when Tanner yelled, "Take ten!" One of the workers with a quad brought everyone drinks and burritos.

Rachel and Rebecca were thankful for the rest. Harvesting was a lot of work and moved at a very fast pace. They were keeping up with Tanner and Ron. Rachel, however, knew they shouldn't be. Tanner had done this his whole life; he had to be slowing down for her. They were, however, moving at a fast-enough pace to keep up with Shawn who was very energetic, helping her not be too worried. No one could keep up with the most experienced pickers. They had been working vines most of their lives and were a lot older than Tanner, but they were extremely fast. They put everyone else to shame. But for Rachel to keep up with Shawn, who had done it many years, made her happy.

"Well, we're keeping up at least," Rebecca whispered to Rachel.

"Yes, but how long can we last at this speed," Rachel gave her a curious look of exhaustion.

"You're not doing half bad," Ron wandered over to Rebecca with his burrito.

"Half bad? I'm keeping up with you," she corrected him.

"Only because I let you," he challenged.

"You're on, Mister," she accepted the challenge. She choked down her burrito, then stood up, wiping her hands together and said, "Let's go, I'm ready."

Ron's face dropped because he had just picked up his burrito and wasn't ready to go back to work yet.

"Hold on, wild woman," Tanner said with a chuckle. "You both need at least five minutes to catch your breath then you can race some more."

"I guess he does, anyway," she pointed at Ron who quickly sat down and started eating his burrito. She protested with an exaggerated sigh, but sat back down on the ground following the boss's instructions. Deep down she could use the five minutes but would never admit it to Ron.

Tanner and Rachel laughed as Ron decided to be quiet for a minute to make sure he got to eat his food.

"How are you guys doing, Shawn and Dave?" Tanner asked as he sat next to Rachel to eat his food.

"We're good," Dave smiled, thrilled to be working next to his friend once more.

"How about you, Shawn," Rachel asked.

"Yeah, I'm good," Shawn said with a forced smile. She noticed he looked a little off and wasn't eating his burrito. Of course, Rachel didn't eat all of hers either. The excitement was too much for both of them, she figured.

Tanner looked at Rachel, sensing that something was up with Shawn. Rachel knew she couldn't embarrass him in front of his friend. They were going to have to keep working and just wait it out. If he's still acting odd by the next break, she'll pull him aside to question him whether it embarrasses him or not.

Everyone worked hard for the next hour and a half. Some, a little too hard, like when Rebecca and Ron had a race picking the grapes down their row. Rebecca kept up with Ron for about six feet then he flew past her. Before long she was yelling to him that he was cheating and she started throwing grapes at him.

"Hey, not the grapes," Tanner yelled to them.

"Don't worry, I was using the rotten ones to throw at that rotten guy," Rebecca teased, knowing she lost the race.

Rachel took off her sweatshirt, feeling overheated. The sun had barely come up and it wasn't very warm yet, but she was hot. Tanner glanced at her and decided it was time for another break.

"Let's take ten," he yelled, and everyone stopped picking grapes again. "You okay?" he asked Rachel as he walked towards her. But before he could reach her, she dropped to the ground like a rock.

Chapter 15

"Rachel!" Tanner yelled, running over to her where she had collapsed. He was only slightly worried about her before, knowing she had never done this kind of work before, but for her to collapse this quickly scared him. Fear shot through him, what could be happening?

"What's wrong?" Rebecca and Ron came running down the row the minute they heard Tanner's shout.

"She just collapsed!" Tanner told them as he shook her shoulder gently, trying to get a response. "Rachel, can you hear me honey?" Her face was pale and he was worried sick.

No response.

"Rachel," Rebecca called out. Her voice shook as she feared for her friend. Standing over her, she wasn't sure if Rachel had just fainted or if she was even breathing.

Tanner checked her neck for a pulse. "She's got a pulse. I knew she was overdoing it! I shouldn't have let her come up this hill."

"She'll be okay," Ron told Rebecca and Tanner, trying to calm their fears. "She's probably just overheated."

"That's the problem, it's not even hot yet," Tanner commented, confused, as he felt her head for a fever. "Who's got some water?" He knew someone would have a bottle. They always kept plenty of water coming for the workers while picking. It was important for everyone to stay hydrated.

"I do," a female worker hurried over, handing Tanner a bottle of water and her scarf to use as a rag. "Thank you, Sofia." Tanner quickly put water on the rag to use on her face and forehead.

"Tanner! Tanner!" Dave came rushing down the row. "Something is wrong with Shawn, he just collapsed. I don't know if he's breathing." Dave stopped in his tracks, shocked, when he saw Rachel on the ground as well.

"What?" Tanner and Ron voiced at the same time. Tanner stood up quickly upon hearing the news. Neither one could believe what they were hearing. *Rachel and Shawn had both collapsed?*

"Stay here with Rachel, I'll be right back," Tanner pulled at Rebecca's hand, guiding her down next to Rachel. He wanted her close to Rachel, keeping a good eye on her. He had to make sure Shawn had a pulse and was breathing.

Ron and Tanner ran to Shawn who also looked pale. Tanner checked to see if he had a pulse and he did. He put his ear down close to his mouth, listening for breathing and watching to see if his chest moved. "He's breathing."

"What in the world is going on? For both of them to suddenly collapse?" Tanner ran his hand through his hair, frustrated.

"Maybe it was something they both ate or drank?" Ron suggested, trying to help keep everyone calm.

Tanner didn't waste any more time. He called 911, reporting that two people had collapsed.

"Let's get that flatbed emptied and get them on it and down the hill quickly," Tanner directed Ron and the other two workers who had hurried over.

"Tanner, Rachel's coming to," Rebecca yelled out.

"Stay with Shawn," Tanner told Dave, "Tell me if there is any change."

Tanner hurried to Rachel, telling her to stay put while she got her bearings. When she was finally able to sit up she looked confused.

"What happened?" she asked, dazed.

"You passed out. How do you feel now?" Tanner asked, still concerned.

"I feel a little sick to my stomach," she put her hand over her stomach.

"The way you got hot suddenly then fainted, maybe you and Shawn both have the flu or something?" Tanner questioned her.

"What do you mean me and Shawn?" She was really confused now. "Did he throw up?"

"He passed out right after you did," Rebecca told her.

"Shawn's coming to," Ron yelled.

"What!" Rachel couldn't believe Shawn had fainted. She tried to get up, worried about Shawn, but Tanner held her back.

"I'll go to him, you stay put!" he ordered her. "You need to take it easy, you might faint again," Tanner warned.

"No Tanner, I have to get to Shawn, he needs me," she was determined. He knew she was right, Shawn would be very frightened after passing out.

"You go slow and easy then. No hurrying!" he ordered, "Rebecca, you make sure she goes slow." He hurried ahead of her to make sure he got to Shawn quickly. He knew how scared he could get.

Tanner could hear sirens coming from a distance.

"Call my dad and tell him what happened," Tanner told the worker who carried a small walkie talkie. Tanner knew his dad would be very concerned when he saw an ambulance drive in and would need to know what was going on, but he didn't want to waste time on the walkie talkie. He had to keep an eye on Rachel and Shawn and get them down the hill quickly and safely.

Shawn was struggling to sit up when Tanner got to him. Tanner was relieved, things couldn't be too serious if he had already come to and was trying to sit up. He was still concerned over what caused the problem, though.

"Take it easy now." Tanner squatted down next to Shawn and reached for his arm to help steady him. "Maybe you should just sit a minute and get your bearings."

Feeling dizzy still, Shawn surrendered his plan to stand and settled for sitting, just as Tanner suggested.

"Do you have any idea why you passed out?" Tanner asked, hoping to get some clue about what was happening with the both of them.

Rachel got there before he could answer and knelt down at Shawn's side. Tanner could see her color was coming back.

"Shawn, what happened? Do you remember passing out?" she asked.

"You said I wouldn't pass out but I just got dizzy and down I went. I didn't even have time to relax or practice anything, I just fainted," he looked up at her, scared and confused. He felt misled that she told him he wouldn't pass out from his panic attacks and now he had. What else could she be wrong about? Insecurities filled his mind.

"She passed out too, Shawn," Dave told him.

"What?" Shawn glanced in Dave's direction at his comment, then back to Rachel. "You passed out too?"

It actually made him feel better that it was probably something different from the panic attacks causing them both to pass out. But then he instantly became worried about Rachel. "Are you okay? Why'd you pass out?"

"Everything is going to be okay," she assured Shawn. "We both probably overexerted ourselves when we're not used to working this hard. Or maybe we both have a virus. At least you didn't pass out from a panic attack."

"Either way, we're going to have you both looked at by a doctor. The ambulance is down the hill waiting," Tanner tried to keep calm but his hands slightly shook. Normally, he keeps it together, but this is his wife that is ill and she means everything to him.

"I'm not going anywhere dressed like this," Rachel argued.

"Yes, you are!" Tanner demanded. "And I'm going with you."

Shawn's color was back, and he felt good enough to also protest going to the hospital, but Tanner wouldn't take no for an answer.

"Tanner, you can't leave now," Rachel warned, worried. She knew how important it was for him to be in the fields right now, especially with his dad already injured. "Shawn and I can go together. You stay here," she suggested as she got on the flatbed.

"Not happening!" he told her firmly. He helped Shawn and Rachel onto the back of the flatbed and rode along with them. He left Ron, Dave, and Rebecca to stay and continue the picking. Rebecca wanted to go along to the hospital, but Rachel insisted she stay and help Ron keep working. She felt bad enough that they already had three less people picking now. "Please Rebecca, I'll be fine. It means more to me for you to be here picking grapes and helping Ron," Rachel pleaded.

"Tanner, you call me if anything is wrong or if she needs me," Rebecca told him sternly.

"I will, don't worry," he promised, knowing how close they were.

Once the EMTs checked their vitals and they were found to be stable, Tanner assured Rachel and Shawn he would meet them at the hospital as he headed for his car. He wasn't allowed to ride in the ambulance with them. Victoria started to climb in the car with Tanner, but he stopped her.

"I need you here Mom, with Dad," he said. At that moment, Neil had come over to get an update. "Or he'll overdo, and we'll have him in the hospital too," he continued, not afraid for his dad to hear.

"I'll take it easy. You take care of them and I'll take care of us," Neil said. Victoria looked up at him with apprehension. "Don't worry, we'll get through this together," he assured her. He was there for her this time and they'd make it through this trauma together.

"I'll take care of these two," Tanner promised as he got behind the wheel and drove off.

Victoria tuned to Neil, voicing her concerns. "Why would they both pass out like that? It's not from the heat. I don't understand."

"Neither one of them are used to the hard work, they could have just done too much. Or maybe they both have the flu. Either way, I doubt it's anything serious," Neil tried to convince her as he started walking her toward the house.

Rachel was worried about Shawn, not herself, as they rode in separate ambulances. She also knew he felt like she had lied to him by telling him he wouldn't pass out from a panic attack and now he was questioning if he had. She knew his state of mind could bring on another attack. Going to the hospital could frighten him enough to bring on an attack. She was feeling more like a mother at that moment than a sister-in-law. She wanted to be with him if he did start to have an attack, but she knew the hospital would insist on checking them out separately. It wasn't that the hospital couldn't take care of him, she just didn't want him to go backwards in his progress.

When the ambulance drove up to the emergency entrance and the staff began wheeling Rachel inside, Tanner was already waiting anxiously.

"I'm okay Tanner, find Shawn and stay with him," Rachel insisted when he rushed over to her gurney.

"I'm not leaving you," he argued. "This is a hospital. They'll take care of him."

"Tanner, if you don't go to Shawn I'll get up off this bed and walk over to him myself, I swear. He needs his brother right now. You were there during his last attack, he has confidence in you. I need you to help him stay calm." She was seriously concerned. She had worked hard to get this family stable and didn't want the whole thing to blow up over this.

"Rachel," he started to protest but he could tell by the look on her face that she wasn't backing down.

"Okay, but you have them come get me the minute you find out anything," he insisted.

Rachel was right, by the time Tanner reached Shawn's room, he was alone and looking bad. His face was pale again and he was starting to sweat. His eyes widened with relief the minute Tanner came through the doorway.

"Shawn, Rachel sent me here to make sure you were doing your relaxation techniques and your proper breathing," When Tanner got close, he could see Shawn was tense. Tanner was trying to think of a quick way to help him.

"Relax those muscles, guy. Don't make me have Rachel come over here and get after you. She's right across the hall, you know," Tanner warned, pointing toward the hallway as if he was about to go get her.

"She said I wouldn't faint." He felt betrayed as if maybe the techniques wouldn't work anymore.

"Rachel knows what she's talking about with panic attacks. I remember hearing her say to you at one time that even if you did faint your body would take over breathing for you and you'd be okay. That's just what happened, like she said. You fainted and your body took over and you're fine," he reassured him.

"Well, that's true," Shawn forgot she had told him that. She didn't say 100% chance he wouldn't faint, she just made it clear that normally he wouldn't. Now he felt more confident again.

"So, get that body relaxed and let's get going on the slow breathing. This is a great place for you to practice and we can tell Rachel how well you did afterwards." Tanner was relieved that he was getting somewhere with his brother. He knew it would make Rachel happy. But deep down, he was worried about both of them. To pass out at the same time was really odd. What was wrong and would it happen again?

Blood tests were being run for each of them, but it would be a while before they would get the results. Tanner had been going back and forth between the rooms to check on Rachel whether she liked it or not. After an hour, the doctor came into Shawn's room.

"Well young man," the doctor dropped his clipboard on Shawn's lap. "You know what this blood test tells me?" he asked with a parental tone. Shawn looked innocently at the doctor then at Tanner, like he didn't have a clue. Tanner watched the doctor with concern.

"No, what?" Shawn was frightened as he looked back at the doctor.

"That like most teenagers your age, you're not eating right. You are anemic and that is likely why you fainted." The doctor turned to look at Tanner now, giving him a relieved smile that meant nothing serious is wrong.

"What's that mean?" Shawn asked, clueless.

"It means that because you've been skipping meals and eating like a bird for months, it's finally caught up with you. If you start eating regular, healthy meals again you'll be fine. If not, you'll keep passing out. Right Doc?" Tanner answered Shawn and then looked back at the doctor.

"That's absolutely right," he smiled at Shawn.

"Can I go back and work the harvest now?" he asked the doctor, fired up again, relieved that the diagnosis was nothing bad.

"I'm going to give you an iron shot and some pills to take home with you. If you promise to eat a good meal in the cafeteria here before you leave and take ten minute breaks in the shade every hour along with plenty of water each time, then I'll okay it. You may get a little dizzy on and off for a few days until you get your protein and iron levels back up, but don't let it worry you. That is, as long as you follow all of my instructions," the doctor warned with a scrunched eyebrow as he picked up his clipboard. "No more skipping meals, got it young man?" he lectured Shawn.

"Yes sir, no more skipping meals," Shawn promised.

"I also want to talk to you about something else," the doctor pulled up his stool and sat down so he wouldn't be towering over Shawn. He wanted Shawn's full attention.

"What about?" Shawn was concerned, as was Tanner, that something else was wrong.

"I've heard a little talk between you, your brother, and his wife as he's been racing back and forth, room to room." The doctor pointed at Tanner as he swung his clipboard in the direction of Rachel's room. "It appears you might be having some very uncomfortable panic attacks, I'm guessing." He looked at Shawn for an honest reply.

Shawn was hesitant, not wanting to discuss it with another doctor. He certainly didn't want to be prescribed more medication. Shawn didn't reply, he just looked at Tanner, hoping he'd help him out of the situation. Tanner felt pressured. He didn't want to betray his brother in any way, yet he'd appreciate it if the doctor had a way to help. Tanner decided to say nothing and leave it between them.

"You know," the doctor began, then paused. "You're what, 17?" He looked at his clipboard to make sure his guess was correct.

"Yes sir," Shawn replied like the proper young man he was brought up to be.

Tanner was proud of him for that.

"My son was just a little younger than that when he went through a similar problem."

Shawn was surprised. He was a doctor, how could that happen in his family?

"I know that look," the doctor caught the arched eyebrow Shawn flashed.

"Yes, I'm a doctor and my son had bad panic attacks. We're normal people too, I know it's hard to believe."

Shawn looked to the ground quickly embarrassed.

"My wife and I got medication for our son, but there aren't very many that teenagers can take safely and sometimes they work and sometimes they don't. In his case, he had too many side effects and couldn't stay on them."

Shawn nodded his head in agreement, having experienced many side effects himself in the past. He was surprised by the doctor's candor.

"We didn't give up, though. We took him to lots of different psychiatrists and doctors and finally one day we found a therapist that made all the difference in the world. He taught my son breathing and relaxation techniques that made such a difference." The doctor smiled, remembering the relief he felt when his son finally had some help.

"My sister-in-law," Shawn pointed towards the room across the way where Rachel was, "has taught me a lot of those techniques. They've helped me a lot," he admitted.

"That's great. Sounds like a wonderful sister-in-law." He looked at Tanner and gave him a grateful smile, pleased that they seemed to be one of those very involved families. Then he looked back to Shawn again. "I can see by everyone's concern that you can still use some more help. Am I correct?" He wanted Shawn to confide in him. That alone would be a big step in his recovery.

Shawn looked at Tanner, who gave no expression to interfere in any way, then back at the doctor.

"I'm not totally better. I still get really scared that an attack might come at any minute and I might not be able to control it again," he admitted, looking towards the ground with shame.

"Good for you for realizing it, son. That's the biggest step right there." The doctor patted his leg, then continued. "One thing that is important for progress, besides the breathing techniques, is just being able to tell someone about what's on your mind. A lot of times we can't do that with family without them getting upset or worried. That's why it's good sometimes to have an outsider you can talk to. The therapist my son went to was so easygoing, my son felt he could talk to him about anything. With doctor-patient privacy, anything you say is between the two of you," he promised. This doctor was a parent who knew the importance of privacy to a teenager. "My son started seeing him once a week and before he knew it, he was right back out there with his friends again."

The doctor stood up from his chair, took a card from the left pocket of his long white overcoat, and held it out to Shawn. "I'd really like to give you his card. Try just one visit, that's all I ask. If you like him then see him again. If not, then you don't have to. I guarantee you'll like him, though. I haven't sent a teenager to him yet that doesn't like him. Sometimes he even gets his whole group of teenagers together and takes them all to a football game. He has a son and daughter of his own so he relates well with the youth."

Tanner was loving this idea. He raised his eyebrows towards Shawn, showing him he thought this was a good idea and this was someone he should listen to.

Shawn too was impressed by the doctor himself and what he was hearing. "Okay, I'll see him once and see where it goes."

Tanner was very proud of him, he couldn't help but put his hand on Shawn's shoulder and say, "Good for you, Shawn."

The doctor gave Tanner a quick look of relief that they had succeeded to get Shawn the help he needs. Tanner gave him a nod of thanks.

When the doctor started to leave the room, Tanner stopped him.

"How about my wife across the hall, Doc? Did you get her blood work back yet?" The doctor's expression went blank.

"I did," he turned to leave the room again and Tanner was beside himself with confusion and distress. "She asked me not to discuss it with you. Said she wanted to talk to you about it herself because you'd be worried and might not handle it well," he told Tanner as he left the room with a concerned look.

"What?" Tanner was terror-stricken inside.

"What's wrong with Rachel?" Shawn was panicked as well, trying to leap off the hospital bed. He had a blood pressure cuff still wrapped around his arm, slowing him down.

"Shawn, wait!" Tanner put his hand up to stop him. "I have to talk to her first, it might be something private. Get dressed, I'll tell you the minute I know something."

"No," Shawn argued as he quickly unwrapped the blood pressure cuff and took it off his arm. She wasn't just a sister-in-law to him but a true friend and hero in his eyes. She had changed and maybe even saved his life. The thought of something being seriously wrong with her overwhelmed him. "I'm not waiting."

"Yes, you are. She's my wife," Tanner declared with a stern voice. He didn't have time to fight with Shawn, he was worried about Rachel. Shawn quickly got quiet, reluctantly respecting his brother's authority.

"I'll be back in a minute," Tanner's voice softened.

Tanner entered Rachel's room and she was nearly completely dressed. *Why is she dressed? If something is this wrong, I'm not letting her leave here.* "Are you okay?" he questioned her, confused. "They're letting you leave?"

"They can't help me any more at this point," she informed him calmly as she put on her shoes.

"What do you mean, at this point? What is wrong with you? Where's the doctor? I want to talk to him," Tanner yanked open the curtain he had just come through. He wasn't playing anymore games, he wanted answers right now.

"They can't help me in here for another seven and a half months or so." An amused look crossed her face.

"What? That doesn't make sense, seven and a half months?" Tanner stopped, confused. His irritated look transformed into a huge smile once it registered. "You're going to have a baby?" he questioned, shocked.

"That's what they say," she let out with a giggle.

Tanner hurried over to her and lifted her off the ground then swung her around in the air. "We're going to have a baby!" he shouted.

"What! What did you just say?" Shawn had come rushing across the hall when he heard his brother's loud voice. He had been straining his ears to hear anything he could about Rachel from his room across the hall.

"I'm going to be a daddy!" Tanner lifted Shawn up in his hospital gown and twirled him in the air, overjoyed. Rachel let out with a chuckle, feeling that if the doctor entered the room right now, Tanner would probably lift him off the ground too.

"What! I'm gonna be an uncle?" Shawn asked as they twirled. They were all three laughing as the doctor came in to see the fun yet also to keep their noise controlled.

Tanner put Shawn down and Shawn hurried over to give Rachel a hug. Tanner shook the doctors hand, wildly and firmly. He was relieved his wife wasn't seriously ill and overjoyed to find out he was going to be a father.

"I wondered why the sight of food was making me ill lately and I was getting tired so easily. The doctor said that's all normal the first few months of pregnancy," she told Tanner.

"Can I call Dad and tell him?" Shawn wanted to spread the news.

"Yes, but tell him not to tell Mom or Rebecca. We want to see their faces when they find out," Tanner said excitedly, twirling Rachel around again.

"You might not want to keep doing that when I get nauseous this easy," Rachel warned with a slight chuckle. He instantly put her down as if she were made of glass.

"Oh, honey, I'm sorry."

She looked at him with a grin. "It's okay Tanner, I'm not going to break, I just get nauseous easily, that's all."

Shawn was getting a big kick out of Tanner. He totally had the 'I'm going to be a dad' syndrome going on.

Tanner was in no hurry to leave the hospital. He had many questions to ask the doctor about his wife's pregnancy. Neither Rachel nor Tanner had planned this exactly. They wanted kids eventually, but they weren't really trying yet. They were too busy getting ready for the harvest and didn't have their own place. They had agreed not to be upset if it should happen, and it was a good thing, because now it had.

After a couple of hours, they finally got to leave the hospital. Shawn had to eat a good meal in the cafeteria before the doctor would release him to go home. Before leaving, they picked up a couple of pacifiers, tied a cute ribbon around each one, and placed them in little gift-wrapped boxes with bows to surprise Victoria and Rebecca.

Chapter 16

Once they arrived at the winery, Shawn was anxious to get back to work with his friend.

"You take it easy now, I don't want any more passing out," Tanner warned.

"Don't worry. The doctor gave me an iron shot and told me to keep drinking orange juice while I work and I should be fine." Shawn ran for the house to get some bottles of juice and to let his mom know he was okay before he went back to the harvesting.

"Rachel, you need to go inside with Mom and get some rest," Tanner hurried over to help her out of the car.

"Tanner, I'm only a couple months along and you're acting like I'm nine months along," she took his hand and let him help her out of the car. "I'm not going to go inside and rest, that's all I've been doing for hours at the hospital. I need to go do some work or I'm going to lose my mind."

"Okay, then cook with Mom. That's work, but not hard labor," Tanner encouraged, as he shut the car door.

"Every time I make food, I get sick to my stomach. No thank you," she replied.

"Oh, boy, this is going to be a long seven months of trying to keep you down," Tanner groaned.

"Yes, it is," she gave him a determined smile.

Victoria came out of the house, hurrying over to check on Rachel. Shawn followed behind carrying his juice, not wanting to miss his mother's face when she heard the news.

"Your dad said you both were okay, but he didn't tell me what was wrong with Rachel?" She watched Rachel closely, trying to detect anything different. Noticing Shawn following her, she turned to give him a quick comment before addressing Rachel.

"You should go back inside and get some food in you," she told him, pointing at the house. She was relieved that Shawn was going to be fine and wanted to keep it that way.

"No, please," he held his hand over his stomach, making an ill face. "The doctor made me eat a big meal in the cafeteria before he'd release me. I couldn't possibly eat more."

"Good, I'm glad. Sounds like a good doctor."

"You have no idea what a good doctor he is," Tanner assured her, planning to tell her later all about Shawn's new therapist. She'll be very pleased. He didn't want to talk about it in front of Shawn and make him feel uncomfortable. No, he didn't want to chance letting anything change his mind about seeing that therapist.

"What about you, Rachel? Are you okay?" Victoria felt very unsettled, as if everyone was keeping something from her and Rachel was seriously ill.

"We brought you a little gift from the hospital." Rachel didn't answer her question, just held out the wrapped gift.

"A gift?" Victoria felt very confused. "That was sweet, but what did they say about you fainting?" At the moment, she was more concerned for Rachel then she was about getting a gift.

"Mom, take the gift. It's important to Rachel," Tanner encouraged.

Victoria reached out, not wanting to hurt anyone's feelings. Rachel placed the gift in her hand. Victoria just stared at it blankly. Shawn, Tanner, and Rachel awaited her response when she finally opened it.

Victoria looked at the pacifier blankly, not understanding. She looked up at Tanner and the minute she saw his proud smile, she knew.

"You're going to have a baby?" she questioned, turning to Rachel.

Rachel nodded her head and Victoria was ecstatic. It was to be her first grandchild. She leaped into the air and hugged Rachel, then Tanner, then Shawn. She wanted to hug anyone around, she was so thrilled. Everyone was laughing. Now Rachel knew where Tanner got his overly enthusiastic attitude.

"Does your father know?" She asked once she could catch her breath.

"I know," Neil came up behind her with a happy grin across his face. "Tanner wouldn't let me tell you, he wanted to see your expression and now I can see why," he laughed, grateful that he didn't miss the moment.

"We're going to be grandparents!" She hugged Neil, then kissed him, still having trouble controlling her excitement.

"Congratulations, son," he put out his good hand, shaking Tanner's hand. He had waited a long time for his family to be together and this happy again.

"Come on, let's go tell Ron and Rebecca," Shawn waved his hand, trying to get Tanner and Rachel to follow.

"We can let Rachel go use the restroom first, she is pregnant remember," Tanner warned, but he was enjoying seeing his brother this enthusiastic. He put his arm around Rachel and pulled her close, giving the top of her head a kiss as he started to guide her inside. He was a happy man and she had a lot to do with it. His parents were back together, his brother was doing great, their best friends were here, and he was starting his own family now. Life was good.

After a short break, they got on the truck for Tony to drive them back up to the area where Ron and Rebecca were still picking. Once they got there, Shawn took off quickly to get to where Dave was picking grapes. Rebecca saw him shoot by.

"Guess he's okay now," Rebecca commented with a snicker as he shot past. She stopped picking to find out how Rachel was doing. Neil had informed them that there was nothing seriously wrong with either of them but didn't fill them in on any details. Rebecca was starting to think maybe it was something of a private nature.

When Tanner and Rachel got out of the truck, Rebecca and Ron had already hurried over to check on them.

"Are you okay, Rachel?" Rebecca asked.

"Yes, I'm fine. I brought you a gift from the hospital," Rachel held out her gift as she did with Victoria.

Rebecca strained to look at Tanner's face to see what they were keeping from her. She looked at Rachel's face, pausing for a moment. Then she blurted out, "You're pregnant, aren't you?"

"What? How did you know?" Rachel dropped her hand that was still holding the gift. "I was trying to surprise you."

Rebecca leaped up and down, rushing over and hugging Rachel. "You're going to have a baby, that's awesome!"

Ron hurried over to congratulate Tanner as Shawn and Dave showed up to see Rebecca's reaction to the news.

"But how did you know?" Rachel was stuck on that thought, even as Rebecca let go of her.

"It was easy! Your husband has a proud smile he's trying hard not to show. The gleam in his eyes alone gave it away. You look slightly nauseous and yet glowing at the same time. That sounds like a proud dad and happy mother-to-be in my books," she explained matter-of-factly.

They all laughed.

"She knew?" She guessed before you told her?" Shawn questioned Rachel, bewildered.

"Yes, you know Rebecca! She's always got to be different from anyone else," Rachel rolled her eyes. She really wasn't upset. It was actually funny to her that her friend could tell.

"It does figure with Rebecca," Shawn chuckled, shaking his head as he told Dave the news and directed him back towards the vines now that the excitement was over.

"What's the gift?" Rebecca put her hand out. Rachel placed it in the palm of her hand. She opened the box. "A pacifier! It's so cute."

"It would have been, if you hadn't guessed it," Rachel snarled, but smiled.

"Looks like you guys have been doing a nice job while we were gone," Tanner glanced around at all the rows they had picked.

"We've been trying, but we're new at this," Ron replied.

"Well we're back now, so let's get back to work," Tanner suggested as he gave his friend a pat on the back.

"Rachel, you take it easy. You're not going to be out here very long at all before I have Tony take you back to the house."

Rachel gave a little protesting moan. "The doctor didn't say I couldn't work, Tanner." She started picking grapes by Rebecca.

"Well I did," he said sternly.

"Am I hearing a Tough Love attitude?" Ron teased Tanner.

"Yes, you are," Tanner joked back. "It's tough on me trying to keep her from doing too much while she's pregnant, because I love her..." his voice trailed off as he walked up the rows of vines.

"How sweet!" Rebecca teased Rachel.

"Right, real sweet," Rachel grumbled.

"What's up Rachel? Something is bothering you, I can tell," Rebecca asked once the men were a good distance away.

"Nothing." But her voice was clearly troubled.

Tanner and Ron went to work farther ahead in the row, knowing the women would want some time to chat privately after the big news. The men were more focused on catching up on the picking.

"Right," Rebecca didn't believe her. "Spill it girl," she insisted.

"I guess my hormones are already affecting me because I'm already feeling depressed."

"Why? Aren't you happy about having a baby?"

"Of course I am, but now I feel like I'm going to be good for nothing when it comes to helping Tanner."

"What do you mean?"

Rachel noticed that Rebecca had definitely gotten the hang of picking grapes while she was at the hospital because she was moving very quickly down the row. Rachel had to pick up her pace to keep up with her.

"He already doesn't want me doing very much and it's only going to get worse from here. I feel like I'm not going to be any help to him for the next seven months. Even once the baby is born, it will be a long time after that before we can work together again like this. Here we just got married and already I'm not going to be there for him," she explained.

"Wow! I think you're right, your hormones are really working overtime," she agreed. "However, let me straighten you out girl. First of all, you're going to have his child and that is the most special thing a woman can do for her husband. You're going to carry it for nine months, then go in labor for hours to deliver it. Believe me, that's doing something for him."

"But it's not the same as working beside him outdoors and helping him out," she countered.

"Once the baby gets a little age to it, you'll be able to get babysitters to help watch the little one while you do some projects with Tanner. You'll have a lot of us around to help, when you think about it. Plus, Beth has an actual daycare which could be very handy."

Rachel was listening as she picked grapes, thinking about her friend's comments. It was helping, but Rebecca could tell she still hadn't totally reached her yet.

"Last, and most important, you need to realize how much you've already helped Tanner," Rebecca assured her.

"What? I've barely done anything and then I ended up in the hospital?" Rachel questioned, confused and irritated with herself.

"You've been a hero to Tanner. A Real Hero, as you call it, and to everyone around here," Rebecca paused her picking to get Rachel's attention.

"What are you talking about?" Rachel really thought she was crazy now.

"What did you teach me a Real Hero was?" she asked. Then she answered her own question: "A Real Hero is not some character in a suit with fake powers, you always say. It is an ordinary person who shows their superpowers through Love and Concern for others." Rebecca looked at Rachel, then over to where Shawn was working.

Shawn was laughing and chatting away with Dave as they raced picking grapes. "What you did with Shawn made you a Real Hero in Tanner's eyes, his parent's eyes, and in Shawn's eyes," she continued. "Tanner is not going to feel like you're slacking on anything for a long time after what you've done for his whole family. You gave him his brother back. You gave Neil and Victoria their son back and by doing so, you even helped to save their marriage."

Rachel blushed. She hadn't really thought about how much it really did mean to Tanner and his family. She was just glad to help in any way she could. When she thought about the joy the family had now, it made her feel good inside.

"Isn't that right, Tanner?" Rebecca yelled out loud enough for Tanner to hear. She wasn't letting this go. She was determined to get Rachel back to feeling like herself again. She couldn't let her go into seven months of pregnancy already feeling useless.

"What's that?" Tanner called out from down the row. Rachel's face turned beet red, worried about what Rebecca was going to say.

"Rachel is a 'Real Hero' don't you agree?" Rebecca needed back-up from Tanner to convince her distraught friend. Tanner stopped picking grapes and walked over to Rachel. Rachel was too embarrassed to even look at him. Tanner took hold of her wrist, stopping her from clipping the grapes long enough to pull her close to him. She couldn't help but look at him now. "She sure is," he gave her that flirtatious smile, making her melt in his arms, then he kissed her. "And this," he added, gently rubbing her stomach, "is our baby hero in here."

"Okay, back to work you love birds," Ron ordered as he came over and got Rebecca.

For the next hour, Rachel was in a good mood, feeling like herself again. Tanner was still in father mode, making lots of plans as they worked side by side.

"Rachel, I've been thinking. With the baby coming, I think we ought to get busy house hunting," he suggested.

"Really? That sounds great but that means you'll be leaving the winery to move back near Crystal Rough, are you ready for that?" She was anxious to buy a house and move back to her hometown, but she didn't want to upset his life plans.

"Once the harvest is all done, they'll do fine without me. Besides, we can drive down here any time they need our help. We need to start getting our own life set up. We're going to have a family soon," he said, charged up.

"That sounds great to me. When do you want to start driving up there to look for a place?" Rachel asked.

"I figure that when you are resting between picking grapes you can start looking for houses online and get a feel for what's out there. The research will take weeks, just narrowing down what area we want to live in, the type of home, and the price range. By the time you know for sure what you want me to look at, I'll be done with the harvest," Tanner explained, wanting to keep her out of the fields and busy house hunting.

"That's true, but what if I find something I want to look at before the harvesting is done?" She placed the bin she had filled with grapes onto the flatbed.

"Don't fill your bin that full. I don't want you lifting that much weight," Tanner lectured her as he put his overflowing bin of grapes on top of her bin.

She rolled her eyes. "Okay, but answer the question."

"That's easy, you can take Mom and go look at the houses. She'd love to spend time with you. Check out the different homes and neighborhoods and when you find the house that you're in love with you can take me to see it."

Rachel was good with that plan, she got along well with his mother. "That's sounds like a great idea," she told Tanner.

Tanner and Rachel were quiet for the next little bit. It was obvious Tanner was thinking about their new child on the way. Rachel, on the other hand, looked like she had a lot more on her mind.

We're buying our own home. I can't believe by this time next year we'll have our own home and our own child, she smiled. I wonder if it will be a boy or a girl? I wonder what we'll name it? I wonder how shocked Beth will be to hear I'm having a baby and moving back near her? Beth! She suddenly realized she hadn't even called her or Aunt Flora to tell them about the baby yet. *I bet Beth will want me to have a girl. I bet Aunt Flora will start knitting me baby clothes and sending them to me. Or will she sew them? She's good at both.* Her mind continued to race as she quickly snipped the grape bundles and they gently fell into her hand. *I wonder whether Ron will stay here at the winery or go back to Florida when we move out?*

She looked at Rebecca and Ron as they were competing again, working their way down each row and trying to show one another up. Their laughter was contagious, and they threw grapes at one another every so often when Tanner wasn't looking. *I wonder if Rebecca and Ron will still be together by the time the baby is born or by the time we move away from the winery. They seem so close right now, but Ron is an unpredictable man, he could leave at any moment.*

She looked over at Shawn who was moving along quickly like the experienced grape picker he was. He and Dave were talking about sports and how Shawn planned to get involved in them again. *I wonder how he'll do with all those people watching him?* Shawn picked up two bins filled with grapes, placing them on the flatbed, while Dave struggled to do the same. Shawn still had those muscles from many years of winery work. She was glad one year didn't take it all away.

I wonder when I'm looking at houses whether I should look for a house in the city or suburbs where we can have animals? Do we want animals? She put her half-filled bin of grapes on the flatbed. Tanner gave her a smile for not over-filling the bin like he had asked. *Tanner loves working at the winery, will he really be happy moving away?*

Cindi Annette

There was so much to think about. She could already feel those emotional hormones kicking in again. *I won't worry about any of these things right now.* She calmed her thoughts, remembering what Aunt Flora used to tell her when she had these types of disquieting thoughts:

Time will tell.

Yes, that's for sure, a year from now and time will have answered all of these questions.

Acknowledgements

I want to thank my very good friend Danielle who works very hard and goes above and beyond to help get these books published. We work hard side-by-side editing each book as well as enjoying every story while we prepare them for publication. Thank you!

Upcoming Book Releases

Would you like a sneak preview of Book 3? Sign up as a subscriber at CindiAnnette.com for a sneak preview and more information on this series. Subscribers will be able to follow along with upcoming events, get free gifts, and find out how to preorder publications to be sent to you right when they come out.

Feedback

If you enjoyed reading this book as much as I enjoyed writing it for you, please tell others about this series and leave feedback on amazon.com to spread the word.

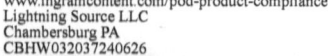